CW01095553

Roll Up for the Arabian Derby

Also by Susan Wicks

fiction
The Key
Little Thing

poetry
Singing Underwater
Open Diagnosis
The Clever Daughter
Night Toad, New & Selected Poems
De-iced

memoir
Driving My Father

Roll Up for the Arabian Derby

Susan Wicks

Published by bluechrome publishing 2008

2 4 6 8 10 9 7 5 3 1

Copyright © Susan Wicks 2008

First published in Great Britain in 2008 by
bluechrome publishing
PO Box 109,
Portishead, Bristol. BS20 7ZJ

www.bluechrome.co.uk

A CIP catalogue record for this book is available from the
British Library.

ISBN 978-1-906061-39-5 hardback

Printed by Biddles Ltd, King's Lynn, Norfolk

Contents

for my family

Water

It must have been in the small hours that it woke me, the swish of it blowing across the fields, drumming on the lane under my attic window, pattering in the leaves of the roses round my back door. A creaking, as if someone were trying to get in. And then something else. I listened. A drip. Soft, half-absorbed by the carpet. And again. And then another, and another, regular as a heartbeat. I felt on the floor for my torch and turned it on. Nothing, as far as I could see. I got up and pulled on a sweater over my nightie. I padded over to the end of the loft, shining the ring of light just ahead of where I was putting my feet. On the far side, under one of the cross-beams, there was a small dark patch. A drop fell from the wood, glittering, and I watched the stain edge out, a few millimetres further. I aimed the torch above my head and the light came back to me, the old oak already darkened by the wet. As I stood there, another drop fell on my head and ran down.

I pointed the torch all round me, across the floor. And there was another patch, a third, a whole series of sinister-looking blotches, the roof at that end obviously quite rotten, peppered with small holes. There was nothing I could do about it. There were too many of them. For a moment I just stood there, shivering, listening to the rain pounding against the house. All around and above me the roof was leaking. I was standing under a giant sieve.

I felt my way to the light-switch at the foot of the stairs. In the sudden glare the downstairs rooms looked ordinary. I found a plastic bowl in the sink, another in the cupboard underneath. A bucket in the bathroom. A couple of saucepans, an enamel casserole. Towels from the chest of drawers. An old grey floorcloth. One by one I lugged them all up that steep stairway and positioned them as well as I could under the drips. I swathed the chimney-breast in old rags, put the bowls under the worst place, towels crumpled in them to deaden the noise. The whole thing must have taken me about an hour. And then I crept back into bed and pulled the covers up over my shoulders. I put my head under the pillow so I wouldn't hear. But the rain on the tiles was still a distant roar. And the rhythm of the dripping was still there – however hard I tried to shut it out I could still hear it quite clearly. The dark patches at the other end of the attic were still spreading. Eventually they would meet and run together into one enormous lake. Little by little it would rise round the legs of my bed until I lifted off like a boat on the incoming tide. Then something above me would give a fraction and a cold torrent would suddenly empty itself over my face.

I rang old Perreaux first thing. He was out already. I spoke to his wife. She said he'd be round in his lunch-break. He'd see what he could do. I told her to tell him it was urgent. I stripped my bed and made up the big one in the bedroom downstairs. Then I sat here at the kitchen table, looking out at the rain as it swept across the valley in a wet grey curtain. I could hear it hitting the side of the house with a slap.

And this morning I can't do anything. Can't write. Can't read. I tried to get down to a letter, but it started turning into a litany, it was pure unadulterated self-pity. In the end I couldn't stand it. I went up into the attic again. The wet patches had dried back a bit, even though outside it was still raining. I emptied the pots and pans and wrung out the rags. Then I sat on the floor cross-legged, right in the middle, the way Paula used to. I sat there, breathing quietly. After a while my ears stopped straining for the little soft sound. It didn't matter any more whether it was raining or whether the whole valley was clear and open in front of me, in full sun.

*

9

When I ring your bell you don't answer at first. I'm standing there on your doorstep like a complete idiot with a Sainsbury's bag full of bread and grapes and French cheeses. Then the door opens and you're frowning at me, as if I've interrupted something. You're wearing your long denim skirt, sandals on your bare feet. You stand aside to let me go through into the hall.

'Are you working?'

'I was.'

'I brought lunch.'

'A comfort package,' you say dryly.

I stand looking at you. 'You haven't got time for comfort.'

You're looking nonplussed.

'Do you want me to leave?'

In spite of yourself you're starting to smile. 'No,' you say. 'No, it's all right. As long as you don't stay more than a couple of hours. Only I do have to work. I'm doing these to a deadline.'

'When?'

'Monday.'

'Right,' I say. 'I'll try not to keep you.' I get out my things and arrange them on the table – bleu de Bresse, tomme de Savoie, Langres, on a little bed of vine-leaves. French bread. A nice bottle of red I brought back from Bergerac. I run into your kitchen for plates, knives, glasses and we eat. Afterwards I wash the few things up and put them away. I look at my watch. 'Well, I think my time's up.'

But you're not telling me to go – not just yet, anyway. You're smiling back and beckoning. Then we're standing in the open door of your darkroom and over your shoulder I can see dark prints floating. You reach to pick one out and show it to me. And as you turn your head I lean towards you and kiss you on the neck.

Someone's knocking loudly on the kitchen door. I turn the key and pull. Nothing happens. I must have double-locked it. I turn the key again, and Perreaux almost falls in on me. He looks as surprised as I am. '*Faut pas salir*,' he says, glancing at me sideways as he makes a show of wiping his boots. 'Show me.' He follows me along the hall and into the loft, hauling his heavy body up the steep steps after mine.

'Here. Here. And here,' I say, pointing at where the rain came in.

He studies the dark patches on the carpet. He reaches up and touches a beam with his finger and mutters something I don't catch. 'Tomorrow,' he says.

I start to plead with him. 'Can't you manage to do it today? Please? Can't you manage to fit me in?'

11

He looks at me with a kind of disgust. 'It's not possible. I haven't the materials. And anyway, it's still raining.' At the front door he holds out his hand to show me. 'Tomorrow,' he says. 'I will come tomorrow. If there is no rain.'

For a long time I couldn't get warm in that big bed. I lay listening to the sounds – a late car passing in the lane, the roses tapping on the glass in the back door, an owl somewhere in the poplars on the hill. And finally I suppose I must have drifted off. Tomorrow he'd come and fix it. He'd bring his ladder and I'd hear him crawling about on the tiles over my head.

And then it started again. I was being pulled out of sleep to the sound of something large and dark beating on the outside wall. And then the dripping, hardly noticeable at first, just the small dull sound of water hitting cloth. And then louder as the water rose in the bucket, ringing as it hit the surface and spattered against the sides. I got my torch and climbed up to investigate, shining the beam into the bowls. The towels were already swimming, the dark patches spreading outwards in places where the plastic didn't quite reach. I altered the positions of the receptacles slightly. Then I backed down the steps and got into bed and tried to go off to sleep again. But however I turned I could still hear the water dripping from the beam to the floor of the attic, just above my face.

This morning I rang Perreaux again. He was there this time. He said it wasn't possible, he'd have to wait for the weather to let up. I spent nearly an hour again wringing out the cloths and hanging them on the clothes-horse in the bathroom to dry. I replaced them with fresh towels from the chest of drawers. I lit the catalytic heater to try and dry everything out, until the windows in every room were thick with steam. I stripped the big bed and made up the couch in the sitting-room. I thought how Paula would have done it. How she would have come up with something to get him moving, something better than this – my book still open at the same page, another abortive letter crumpled in the waste-basket. Paula wouldn't have let it get to her, she'd have found a way to cut straight through. If she were here now she'd take one look at me steaming away gently in my Chinese laundry and start to laugh.

When I ring your bell you don't answer at first. I stand there on your doorstep with my bag full of bread and grapes and nice cheeses. You open the door, half-frowning. 'Come in,' you say finally. You stand to one side and I go past you, into the hall.

'Are you working?'

'I was.'

'I brought lunch.'

'So I see,' you say dryly. 'Well, as long as you don't stay more than a couple of hours.'

I get my things out and arrange them on the table. The cheeses, on a little bed of vine-leaves. A Bergerac I brought back last year. I run into your kitchen for the plates and cutlery and glasses. Afterwards I clear up. I'm trying to smile.

But you're not telling me to go. You're looking at me. We're standing just inside the closed door of your darkroom, our eyes slowly adjusting to the faint amber glow. You've got a proof-sheet in your hand, something scribbled on the white border. You select an image and find the matching negative. Then you slip the dark strip into the holder, the pale blur in the centre framed in metal – a strange hand-mirror, a small carnival mask. You're putting your eye to the grain-magnifier, getting the focus exactly right. Your skin, your hair, everything, dark and close. As you bend your head I lean over and kiss you on the side of your neck. And you turn to me. Amber light. Darkness. You make a small adjustment and straighten your back. You set the timer to five seconds. For five seconds exactly I see you clearly.

Fucking Perreaux. He won't give an inch. When I rang him again his wife wouldn't even let me speak to him – said he was out on a job, renovating a bathroom somewhere, some indoor thing. I was so mad I almost shouted. But what good would it have done? He'll come when he's ready. That's what you learn, finally, as you get older. You can't ever make anyone do anything, can't even make anyone hear you if they don't want to. If he feels like coming and mending your roof for you, he'll do it. If he doesn't, you can drown like a rat. You might as well sit at the edge of the waves and order the sea to go back where it came from. You might as well lie down in the water and let the waves wash over your face.

Better. Last night the rain seemed to be letting up. One or two showers, but from here I couldn't hear much. The dripping wasn't directly above me any more. I probably did manage to get a few hours' sleep.

And this morning I've started another letter, something a bit more cheerful. Outside the sun's actually shining, would you believe. The world's my oyster, which I with sword, etc. I can read, write, go for a walk, anything. Cloud-shadows across the valley. Cuckoos everywhere like an echo, the young poplar-leaves shivering. Even the old collapsed barn looks beautiful, down there on the far bank of the stream. And mid-morning, just when I'd stopped expecting him, who should turn up but old Perreaux with his truck and his ladder and enough tiles to cover the whole roof several times over. I almost hugged him. 'Today,' he said. 'I will have it finished for you today.' I just stood there grinning. He must have thought I was a complete idiot. I waited until I could hear his ladder grating on the front wall, and then the sound of him clambering across to the chimney. Then I grabbed all the cloths and towels from the clothes-horse and pegged them out in the wind and the sun like a row of flags.

I don't believe this. All yesterday afternoon he spent crawling over my roof, farting about with tiles and a bricklayer's trowel, a little mound of ready-mix cement right next to the front door where the crocuses were. And this is it, this is the glorious result. It was two in the morning when the storm hit – in the light of my torch I could just see the face of my watch. A rumble of thunder, coming closer. And then the sound of water running somewhere over my head.

I pulled myself up to the attic. The power had been cut and all I could see was what my torch could show me. From the cross-beam, a silver glitter – not drops, but a small continuous trickle. Patches across the carpet, at both ends; water coursing down the side of the chimney-breast in a thin stream; water dripping even at the other end, where three nights ago I was trying to sleep. The carpet reflecting light, covered by a sheen of water in places, where the pile wasn't deep enough to absorb it all.

Downstairs, drips everywhere – in the bedroom, over the sitting-room doorway, dark streaks reaching across the ceiling. A brown finger over the couch, a brown mark in the centre of my pillow. Flakes of fallen plaster on the pages of my book, a little heap of something like gravel in the bathtub. Snail-trails of dirty water following my bare feet along the hall.

There wasn't anything I could do. I bundled up my bedding and carried it out of the back door, through the little outside door in the wall and down the stone steps to the cellar. Rolled up against the back there was an old strip of carpet. I spread it on the dirt floor and sat down, pulling the quilt up round me, my torch resting on last year's sack of carrots, giving out a thin tube of light. Milk, a few biscuits, an apple. My book. Paper to start a letter, if the spirit should move me. Paper to finish a letter, if I could only think what to say.

When I ring your bell you don't answer straight away. I'm standing on your doorstep with my arms full. And though you don't show it, I can tell you're glad to see me. You take the stuff from me and pull me inside.

After we've eaten you're showing me something. We're in the darkroom. You've got a proof-sheet in your hand, something scribbled in the margin – a date – this time last year. You're laying it flat against the light, you're studying each frame through a magnifier, making up your mind which image you really want to use.

You're doing a test-strip, in five-minute increments. You're watching something surface in a shallow bath of developer, comparing shades of grey. And then the image itself. Stop-bath, fixer, your face almost sleepy with concentration under the amber light. I lean to kiss your neck. You turn and kiss me back, your tongue in my mouth. Which of us is the first to touch the other? I'm not sure. My hands between the wings of your collar, yours up under my shirt. Your nipples like berries, mine flat and soft, changing under your fingers. A ribbon of dark film unrolling underfoot, acetic acid, the grain-magnifier crashing, its small lens spidering like a windscreen where the stone hit. Five seconds? Ten? Fifteen? When you turn on the light I see you standing with your back against the closed door, trying not to smile. Am I the one to reach forward to pick the gleaming print out of the water? Or do we leave it there, half-floating? It's the old barn down by the stream, already collapsing, beautiful. Two women standing in the open doorway, one of them slightly blurred, as if she's only just stopped moving, the lower half of their bodies in full sun. And the sky above them cloudless, the shadows of the young poplars peppering the roof like little moving holes.

Roll Up for the Arabian Derby

The first thing that greeted them as they walked into the camp was the absurd jingle. It was far too loud. But there was something jaunty about it. In spite of herself, Jenny found herself humming it under her breath. And it was obviously working on the children too. Emma forgot she'd ever been whining and started to clap her hands. And Tom was already pulling on Jenny's arms, urging her forwards to where the noise was.

She put the cases down at her feet. The palms of her hands were lined with sweat and dirt from the journey. She straightened her back and stretched. The kids had already run off to where a little crowd had gathered in front of some kind of low building with an awning. The people's backs were towards her and she couldn't see what they were looking at. She strained to keep track of Tom and Emma as they ducked and squirmed, finding their way between the larger bodies, worming their way cleverly to the front.

She heard cheering. Then the jingling music started up again, a man's voice shouting over it, calling out something she couldn't hear properly. A few moments of quiet. And then the jingle came again.

She picked up the two cases and heaved them nearer, until she was only feet away from the edges of the little crowd. From a distance she'd taken the watchers for adults. But most of them were just kids, or teenagers. She could see between and over them, right to the back of the booth.

At first glance, it seemed to be a shop. There were soft toys everywhere, water-pistols, plastic windmills on sticks. A pack of brown furry monkeys tumbled in a net suspended from the ceiling, a tail hanging here and there between the meshes. A giant stuffed panda was tied to the central pole, balloons on either side. One of them had gone down, a little bag of wrinkles. She thought she could hear money changing hands.

But there was something else. The kids were excited, bobbing up and down, shouting – they were doing something at the counter. And on the back wall something was moving jerkily across, from right to left. From here she couldn't quite make out what it was.

She left the cases where they were and edged closer till she was almost a part of the group. She could feel the surge of excitement, see the hands aiming the chutes and feeding in the white balls, she could sense the tension as the players waited for them to roll back. And now she was close enough to make out what the moving things were, on the far wall. They were camels – wooden cut-outs in different colours, each in a separate, numbered groove. She fixed her eyes on one of them. It loped a few mechanical paces and stopped. Then it loped on a few more and stopped again. She clenched her fists involuntarily as it stood motionless while several of the others caught up and overtook. One poor camel hadn't managed to move from his mark at all.

The race ended. The winner pocketed some kind of token. Then the man behind the counter reached up and unravelled a soft toy and handed it over. 'Roll up! Roll up for the Arabian Derby!' he shouted. She thought she saw a few coins pass from hand to hand. And the jingle came, even louder now that she was so close to it, far too loud. Yet she went on standing there, almost as if something inside her were waiting for the man to shout 'Roll up!' and the tinkly music to begin.

A cheer went up and some of the children at the counter moved away. Tom and Emma were still there at the front. They were holding hands. The man was leaning out to take money, giving change, emptying plastic chips out of a little pouch. He leaned towards her children. 'You wanna play?' She saw Emma shrink back slightly, closer to her brother. The man looked up briefly and Jenny caught his eye. It was the lined face of a heavy smoker, slightly seedy-looking, with a little dark moustache and greying hair. Something flashed in the open neck of his shirt, some kind of chain glinting. She looked away. 'Tom! Emma!' she called. In a moment they were skipping round her, the heat and tedium of the day's long journey forgotten. She picked up the cases and together they moved off down the path.

Every morning after breakfast, as they made their way from the dining-room, it was the same tune they heard. Tom and Emma would cling to her hands, begging her for her loose change. And then they'd run forward, Tom's dark head and Emma's fair one bent over the counter side by side, Tom dancing from one foot to the other with excitement as he aimed the chute and fed in the ball. They'd decided number seven was lucky, that the blue number seven camel loped along faster than the others, and won more often. And in fact Tom was steadily amassing tokens. The man knew him by name now. Every morning when he saw him pull free of Jenny and run to the counter his grey face would break into a smile.

It was crazy. Everything else in the camp was free. For days they hung listlessly about the funfair, as she urged the children to try everything – the dodgems, the old-fashioned roundabout with the painted horses, the dragon-train, the flying saucer – until she could have taken a giant metal-crusher to it all. She bought them hotdogs. She bought them candyfloss, the pale strands of sugar shrinking when they bit into them, turning to hard pink clumps.

And the three of them would walk back to the rooms, Tom and Emma whining and dragging their feet. And as they followed the path back across the camp, the jingle would come to them in gusts on the wind. 'Roll up, roll up for the Arabian Derby.' And the children would start to walk faster. They knew what it was the man was shouting, even without hearing the words. He'd grin at them sideways as they went past. Above him the giant panda would sway slightly in the breeze. And the jangle of the music would follow them back to their rooms. The kids hummed snatches of it sometimes. Once Jenny woke in the night, still hearing it through her dreams.

Something must have woken her – some drunk singing or laughing or raising his voice in an argument. She sat up in bed and reached for her watch. By the dim light from the outside stairway she could just read it – 1.30. Everything was as it should be – the square grey room, the lighter grey of the TV screen, the glint of the electric kettle. She could hear the children breathing quietly on the other side of the wall. She lay back on the pillow, her brain still chasing a snatch of the Arabian Derby man's tune.

How had she let it happen? It wasn't her fault they'd arrived half-dead with the heat, hungry and thirsty after the train; that they'd stood waiting for two hours in the hot reception hangar, up where the buses unloaded; that when they'd finally been told where to go the Arabian Derby man had been there to welcome them in person with his little moustache and grey smile.

They began to work out a little routine. The children would run into Jenny's room quite early and sit on the big double bed. She'd drag herself from sleep and put on the kettle for tea, making it very weak, so Tom could have some. Emma would have a carton of orange-juice. They'd dip biscuits in, laughing when a piece broke off and sank to the bottom. The children would bring their toys and books into Jenny's bed. It was almost as if they'd never had to leave their home surroundings at all.

Then Jenny would try to get Tom and Emma to do things. After breakfast she'd take them to one of the swimming-pools – the 'tropical' pool with the wave-machine, where parents sat drinking behind giant cheese-plants, or the pool with the water-slides. Neither was any good for swimming lengths in, but she'd hoped Tom and Emma would like them. And they did, quite. When she went in the water with them, when she laughed and sang and made up games for them, they were perfectly happy. But if she tried to sit at one of the plastic tables, they'd lose interest. The wave-machine frightened them. The water-slides were boring. The moment she opened her book Tom and Emma would be there beside her, shivering, asking if it was time to get out. She'd look up at the tangle of giant, multi-coloured intestines looping across under the glass ceiling. Then she'd take the children's hands and together they'd climb the dripping steps, trying each slide in turn, till she was sure they couldn't possibly be nervous. And then she'd give in and pick up the wet towels and they'd go back to their rooms, where Tom and Emma could play or read, as they did when they were at home.

One rainy afternoon they went to a film-show. In the film, people dressed as huge turtles fought one another, trapping one another in underground car-parks or cellars. The picture was so dark they could hardly make out what was happening. Sometimes all they could see was the light glinting on the armour-plating of the turtles' backs. Emma went to sleep, sucking her thumb. After a while even Tom leaned over to Jenny and whispered, 'Mum, can we go back and play?' Quietly the three of them slipped out of their seats and up the dark aisle to the exit.

Outside, the afternoon was still grey. As they emerged from the film-theatre, a uniformed camp official was passing. He gesticulated and shouted something. Emma jumped and started to cry. Jenny picked her up, stroking the wet hair gently back from her eyes. It was probably just the way these people were trained to say hello.

It was always the number seven chute they ran to. The blue number seven camel loped gracefully across in its groove, hardly ever stopping for more than a few seconds, then galloping away across its landscape of sand-dunes, often the first to reach the far side. The grey man's moustache would twitch. He'd wink at Tom as he handed over another token. He'd do something with his hand under the counter – pull a hidden lever or press a button – and the camels would be yanked back to the beginning, ready to start again.

Every morning, on their way to the other amusements, they'd stop at the booth. And every evening, on their way back. If number seven was taken, they'd stand watching, waiting until it was free. And then the Arabian Derby man would beckon them forward. He'd call Tom by name, smiling in a special way. He probably knew exactly how many tokens Tom had. There was a whole pile of them now back in the children's room, on the bedside table, neatly stacked like a pile of coins. From time to time the man pointed up to the monkeys in their net, raising his eyebrows, but Tom would shake his head.

And the man would laugh, his face creasing into something that was almost a sneer, the little moustache lifting to show his teeth.

*

One morning, when Jenny picked up the children's dirty clothes from the floor of their bedroom, the pile of tokens was missing. 'Tom?' she said. 'Tom?'

Then she remembered – they'd run on ahead of her, to take possession of the number seven pitch before someone else got to it. She locked the door quickly behind her. She hurried along the outside gallery and down, her feet ringing on the iron stairs.

At the booth the crowd was only just beginning. But as she got closer people were already pouring in – teenagers, kids in heavy boots with spiked hair and tattoos, little ones like Tom and Emma, a few adults, their nylon parkas open and flapping in the wind. She squeezed through, and gasped. There was Tom with the man, on the other side of the counter, the man's arm raised above his head in what looked like some sort of crazy gesture, and Tom reaching up too, his small body almost touching the man's.

She could see them clearly now. As she watched, the man untied the giant panda from its pole and handed it to Tom. Tom hugged it to him, grinning. Balloons bumped and floated away along the path, a couple of shrivelled ones rolling, stopping, caught in the tangled trunks of a bush.

She called. 'Emma! Tom!' They came racing to her, Tom almost hidden behind a black and white mass of fake fur. She caught at their hands and dragged them away, past the painted shed that was the film-theatre, past the corrugated structure of the tropical pool with its transparent roof, past the spiralling red and blue tubes of the water-slides, past the gates of the funfair where the dragon-train was on its last lap, letting out its final descending shriek. They walked out through the front gates. They crossed the road to the beach and sat down on the damp shingle, the four of them in a line – a woman with two children and a giant panda – facing the sea.

They walked along the promenade to where a small concrete jetty stuck out into the water. The sun was trying to break through. Emma was running and jumping, finding stray shells and bits of polished glass in the stones scattered over the path. Down on the beach the waves broke noisily, crashing open in a burst of spray that drowned out the noise from the camp. Farther out, the sleek green water swelled and hollowed and swelled again. Gulls screeched over their heads. At the edge a black dog was barking at nothing, a man was throwing sticks. Tom was panting now, lagging behind, the panda almost too big for him to carry. Jenny took it from him and the two children ran ahead, waving their arms and shouting to each other, their voices torn away by the wind. They went right to the end of the jetty and looked over, at the green sea that tilted and churned against the concrete. From time to time a wave broke in a sudden explosion of spray and fell back with a slap, the water streaming. On the far side, a group of fishermen were huddled in boots and dark waterproofs. When she caught the children up they were leaning to peer into the buckets, squealing when they thought something moved. It was nearly lunchtime already. In the dining-room their places would be laid and waiting.

They had lunch at a pub at the landward end of the jetty. The sun was fully out now. They sat in the shelter of the pub wall, at one of two little metal tables. She bought cokes for the children, a half of lager for herself, fish and chips for all three of them. The panda sat stiffly on his own metal chair, his black-ringed eyes staring out towards the sea.

At the other table were a couple of men in waterproofs – fishermen. They were eating fish and chips, too, and drinking pints of something that might have been cider. After a while they pushed back their plates and lit cigarettes. One of them leaned back, resting his head against the sunny wall and smiling, half-closing his eyes. He was smiling at Jenny. The children had gone to sit a few yards away, on a flight of steps that led down to the beach. They sat with their heads close together, the wind making rosettes in their fine hair. 'Nice kids.' The man jerked his head in their direction. He tilted his glass and the yellow liquid flowed backwards into his mouth.

Jenny smiled back.

'You on holiday here?'

'Just for a week.'

'Guest-house?'

'No,' she said.

The man laughed. 'Not at the camp, are you?'

'Yes, actually.' She followed the direction of his eyes and started to laugh with him. 'My son won it this morning.'

'I wouldn't have guessed.' He picked up his glass again and emptied it. 'That's what you all do there, is it? Spend all day at the fair?'

She looked at him. 'Haven't you ever been inside?'

He shook his head, still smiling. 'Never really had the chance. Don't even see much of the people. No idea what happens in there really. Could be one long wild party for all we know.'

The beer slipped down nicely, cool and refreshing. It was good to be out like this, in the fresh air, talking to someone. She filled her lungs. 'Doesn't it affect you at all?'

'Oh...' He was thinking about it. 'Sometimes there's a fight in the town, people getting drunk – staff on their night off, probably. But otherwise you'd hardly know it was there. People get unloaded from buses and go in through the gates, and we never see them. It's a different world.'

'It *is* a different world.' Down on the steps the children were making little patterns with stones, completely absorbed.

'We don't see anything,' the man said.

'But you must hear something?' Jenny turned and looked into his eyes.

'Not really.'

'Nothing?'

'Not really,' the man said again. He turned to his companion for corroboration and the other man nodded. 'Well, I hope you enjoy the rest of your holiday.' He pushed back his chair, making Tom and Emma look up. He waved to them and they waved back.

'Time to go!' Jenny called to them. She made them put on their anoraks and they filled the pockets with stones. She went to pick up the panda.

'No!' Tom's small face was full of anxiety.

'What do you mean, *No?* Someone's got to carry him. And you're all sandy. Look at you!'

'No,' Tom said again. 'Don't.'

'Are you going to carry him?'

Tom shook his head. 'I want him to stay here, on this chair, where he can see the sea.'

'But you can't do that.' Jenny glanced at Emma. The little girl's eyes had filled with tears.

'Why not? He's mine. I won him. I can do what I like with him. And I want him to stay and look at the sea.'

'Well...' She shrugged. She was tired now. They all were. She picked Emma up and carried her in a piggyback as far as the ice-cream van. She bought them both ice-creams. As they ate them they turned once to see if they could still see the panda. The two children pointed, forgetting for a moment to lick, the pink drops running down over their fingers. She could still make out something, a soft rounded shape slumped on a chair in front of the wall.

When the three of them turned in at the camp gates, almost the first thing they heard was the jingle. Its jauntiness was infectious. 'Roll up, roll up for the Arabian Derby!' the man was saying. Emma seemed to forget she'd ever been crying and ran forward, clapping her hands.

Pigs

It's Noddy who's taken it on himself to divide up the bread. He's on his feet, leaning across the refectory table with a long serrated knife in his hand. He steadies the loaf with his left and saws with all his strength. The crust's flaking as the wedge-shaped slices pile up at the cut end. He passes them across to us on the tip of the blade.

We all just help ourselves without bothering to say thankyou. Jeff's busy pouring the wine, sharing out the stingy ration as well as he can between us. James bites straight into his slice, like he was starving. Kim stretches out her hand silently for the bread-knife. When Noddy passes it over she holds it horizontally and cuts her own doorstep neatly in half, the palm of her hand pressed flat to stop it slipping. By the time she looks up Noddy's sitting down again. We all reach across and clink glasses. 'Well, that's that,' Noddy says.

'Bloody good thing!' Jeff lifts his glass to the carved wooden crucifix on the wall. 'If they had to subject us to all that group shit, they might at least have chosen somewhere a bit more... '

'Too right.' Kim helps herself from one of the big pots they've placed at intervals down the centre of the table. Something that looks like brown porridge. She pushes it across in my direction and hands me the ladle. 'I've got all that secondary provider stuff coming out of my ears. Experiential learning, my arse. Self-regulating bollocks. Who do they think we are?'

'Some of them actually go for it,' I say. 'They really do.'

'Bollocks.' Noddy's spreading chilli on his bread with a knife. He folds the slice in half and stuffs it in his mouth. 'It's just the PC thing. They've all got to be seen to be toeing the line. Today experiential turkey-boning, tomorrow nose-flutes or holistic self-abuse.'

'You do talk a load of crap sometimes,' I tell him.

'And why hold it here?' Kim says. 'Why here, for Christ's sake? There must have been hundreds of places.'

'Because it's near?'

'Because it's cheap?' Jeff leans along the table to reach an abandoned half-empty bottle. He refills his glass. Behind us a brown-robed monk moves discreetly. 'Because it's fucking cheap!' Jeff almost shouts it, his cheeks bulging, his face flushed and spurting crumbs.

36

'All right,' I say. 'So it's cheap. I think we've established that. And anyway it's over. We've done our experiential bit. Tomorrow morning we can all go home.'

'Actually,' James says.

We all turn and look at him. His thin face looks even younger in the sideways light from the window.

'Actually, it wasn't all that bad.'

'The place?'

'The place, the food, the people, everything. Even the course itself.'

'Oh, come on!' Noddy says.

Kim joins in. 'But you're not really saying...? James? Are you?'

'It's like Judy says.' He looks across at me and smiles. 'The thing is, some people do honestly believe in it.'

I'm smiling at him. 'Yeah?'

'What the fuck's the matter with you two?' Jeff says. 'What's the fucking point of coming on a fucking thing like this if you're going to start taking it fucking seriously? You might as well have stayed at home and got it out of a fucking book.'

'Thank you, Jeff.' I hold out an imaginary microphone to James, 'I don't know if you'd like to make a comment at this time?'

But Noddy's pushing back the bench. It judders under us on the stone floor, then falls over with a crash. At the far end of the refectory one of the monks turns round, startled. But already we're moving away towards the door. I brush breadcrumbs from my skirt with the flat of my hand. We walk quickly towards the bar. Above the entrance, another carved figure on another cross presses his bony knees together and closes his eyes.

Noddy leans back in the old leather chair, looking up at the ceiling. 'What it needs, all this...' His voice is slurred. He makes an airy gesture towards the half-empty room, the lighted cigarette sending out little staccato puffs.

'What?'

'What it needs...'

'Oh, give it a rest.' Kim looks up from making one of her roll-ups.

'What it really needs,' Jeff says, 'is to lighten up a bit.'

'Meaning?'

'Lighten up. Not take itself so fucking seriously. Give some of these fucking arseholes something to laugh about for once.'

For a moment no one says anything. The smoke's making my eyes water. 'I think perhaps it's time I...'

'No, wait, Jude, don't go!' Noddy's hand's on my arm, stopping me from leaving. 'Don' desert us! We're only just getting going.'

'That's what I'm afraid of.'

'No, seriously, Judy, don't leave. You haven't even heard the one about the man who worked at the abattoir.'

'No, and I don't want to.'

But he lets me have it anyway. And the one about the pneumatic drill, and the one about the woman with dyslexia. And Noddy joins in, the two of them trying to outdo each other, the empty pint glasses multiplying steadily, covering the whole table, clinking together every time one or other of us laughs. And finally Jeff's sitting back in his chair, his big legs crossed at the ankle, a shred of tobacco quivering on his lower lip. And Noddy's bent over his pint, his elbow in a pool of spilt dregs, not really listening, not really even with us. Behind us the room's gone quiet. Everyone except us disappeared long ago. 'I'll tell you one,' I say.

Beside me I hear James's chair creak. Kim's looking at me from under her fringe, her tongue frozen in the act of licking the gummed edge of the cigarette-paper. 'Hang on a minute,' I tell them. I cover my eyes for a moment with my hands. 'Let me just get it straight in my own head before I begin.'

I take my hands from my eyes. In front of me there's a picture over by the window − a robed figure against bleeding clouds. 'Okay,' I say. 'So there was this guy who had this herd of pigs.'

Kim prompts me. 'A herd of pigs.'

'And they happened to be all female. Sows. So there weren't ever any piglets. The guy hadn't got a male pig – boar – to...'

'Yeah, yeah.' Jeff crosses and uncrosses his legs in the low chair.

'So he goes to this friend of his and he says, look, I've got all these pigs, and they're all female and I don't know what to do to get them... '

'Pregnant,' Noddy says.

'And he asks the guy what he ought to be doing and the guy says...'

Jeff's face stretches itself momentarily out of shape in a yawn.

'And he says, well, what you do is you take them all out into the centre of the forest and then you bring them back again, and you'll know if they're – you know...'

'With pig,' Noddy says.

'...because the next morning they'll start to go sort of wild.'

James is looking at me intently. 'What do you mean, "sort of wild"?'

'Well...' I'm frowning, trying to concentrate. 'They'll start to – you know – grunt and squeal and all that. Roll about on their bellies in the mud.'

'Good for them,' Kim says.

'And so the guy loads up his herd of pigs into the back of his truck and drives them all out into the forest, and he does his bit with them...'

Jeff's frowning. 'He does his what?'

'His bit – you know – because he doesn't understand, right? He doesn't realise he doesn't actually have to... '

'Got you,' Noddy says.

'So the next morning he gets out of bed and rushes to the window, all excited, to see if they're rolling about in the mud.' James is looking at me sideways, under his eyebrows. 'And of course they're not. They're looking totally normal. So the next day he loads them all into the back of the truck again and drives off into the woods, and this time he does it even more thoroughly. It takes him more or less the whole day. And the next morning he drags himself to the window and there they all are again – perfectly quiet and contented, not one of them rolling or squealing. And the poor guy's getting really depressed...'

Jeff yawns again. 'How much more of this is there?'

I feel myself start to blush. When I go on my voice is shaking slightly. 'So he loads them all up into the truck again, and drives off into the forest. And this time he does each pig more than once. He does each of them three times – four times, even. It takes him all day and part of the night as well. By the time he's ready to go home it's so late he can hardly find his way back in the dark.'

Noddy breathes out. 'Oh, get on with it.'

'And when he wakes up the next morning, he's like this little old man, all bent up and worn out and aching all over. He can't even manage to get out of bed.'

'Can't even get out of bed! My God!' Jeff opens his eyes wide. He lights a fresh cigarette from the stub of the one before.

'And his friend, who's there – '

'Conveniently.'

'Goes to the window for him, and the guy calls out, Well, what are they doing? Are they starting to behave at all oddly? And the friend says yes, they are. So what are they doing? Are they rolling about in the mud? And the friend says well no, not rolling in the mud, exactly. They're all squashed into the truck. And several of them seem to have climbed into the front seat. And one of them's actually leaning with all her weight on the horn.'

There's a silence. Noddy's staring vaguely in the direction of the painting, not even listening. The others look at me, their faces blank. 'Oh,' Jeff says finally. 'Is that it? It's the way you tell them, Jude. Ha, ha. I've never heard anything quite so funny in my life.'

James stands up suddenly. 'I think I'll just get a breath of air.'

Jeff shakes his head, muttering. He crushes his cigarette out in the full ashtray. 'Judy, has anyone ever told you you're wonderful?'

'Frequently,' I say.

'And I love you,' Jeff says. 'Have I ever told you that?'

I stand up. James has already gone, disappearing into the darkness. 'Hey, James, you arsehole, you can't leave now.' Noddy looks at me, his face heavy with booze and sleep. 'How can you be so heartless?'

The tears come suddenly to my eyes. 'I don't believe... '

And Jeff's suddenly on his knees, his arms round my legs, his head pressed against the side of my ankle. 'It's your feet! You've got such delicious little feet, such touching feet! He leans down towards the carpet and kisses my sock, where it wrinkles at the ankle. 'Hasn't anyone ever told you what touching little feet you've got? A real joke-teller's feet...'

I almost kick him away. But I don't. I'm laughing with embarrassment. I disengage myself as gently as I can from his arms and push out between the chairs and tables to the door.

Outside it's cool and clear, the trees casting their shadows across the dew on the grass. As I walk I'm making a diagonal line of footprints. Along the drive the lights are out. There's only the spill of yellow from the house, one or two windows still lit upstairs, the downstairs rooms blazing. And above me the stars. I put one foot in front of the other, letting my body take me where it wants to. At the big oak tree I stop and listen. A sound like breathing in the leaves as the night air moves through them. The little cold points of light above me flicker on and off.

I sit down, my back against the trunk. I stretch out my legs between the roots, bury my face in my arms and breathe in: through the smoke-stink of my sweater, the faint smell of my own skin, and under it the scent of night on grass. I move slightly and my foot knocks against something. A vodka bottle. I lean forward and pick it up. It glints in the faint light from the sky. 'James?' I say.

From the other side of the trunk a denser shadow leans towards me. 'You mustn't take any notice.'

'I don't. What they need...'

'Is to be driven out into some forest somewhere and just dumped.' He reaches to take the bottle out of my hand, lifts it to his mouth and takes a swig. 'I liked the way you told it.'

'What do you mean? How did I tell it?' I can just see the whites of his eyes gleaming.

'Like that. Like someone who takes jokes seriously. Like someone who's not just waiting for the punch-line, not playing to the gallery, not just telling it for the applause.'

'I don't believe in the gallery,' I say. He leans against me and I rest my head on his shoulder. 'And there was never going to be any applause.'

'I applauded.'

'I didn't notice.'

Over there, above the trees, the stars shimmer slightly as heat escapes from the earth. He holds the bottle out to me in the dark, 'Do you want some?'

'Go on, then,' I say. 'Give it here.' I unscrew the cap and tilt the neck to my mouth. I almost choke. 'It's water!'

'What else?' He raises his hands slightly, palms upward. I can hear the corners of his mouth smiling at me in the dark.

Or

Or you could have done it differently. The moment you heard the car draw up, you could have been down there in the hall, your face wreathed in smiles, your arms already stretched out in welcome. You could have hugged Rebecca, you could have let her see you missed her − nothing else, just that you'd missed her, as any father misses his grown-up daughter. You could have taken a couple of steps forward towards the front door and shown them how eager you were to help. You could have looked Ben in the eye and shaken his hand.

You wouldn't have minded it then, the way the two of them glanced at each other sideways with something that was − and wasn't quite − a laugh. You could have come out with some inoffensive platitude, some innocuous thing about life and Oxford that they couldn't turn back against you. You could have called Annie in from the kitchen, and the two of you could have stood side by side, trying to seem only pleased and interested, trying not to bombard them at once with questions. You could at least have tried to keep the sarcasm out of your voice.

You wouldn't have made that remark then about the luggage. If Annie wasn't complaining about the bag of dirty laundry, why the hell would it matter to you? Or if you *had* said something, it would have come out more like a proper joke, and one or other of the three of them would surely have had the grace to laugh. You might not even have noticed Ben's hair then, that pale, grotesque straggle down over his shoulders. Or Rebecca's sagging jeans with the knees all grey with dirt, the dark rings under her eyes. You'd hardly even have heard his voice, those slimy upper-crust vowels that set your teeth on edge. You'd just have heard what he said, and understood that it was only friendly and actually quite sensible. You wouldn't have been so aware of all those generations of privilege, Eton collars and public speaking and sherry in the housemaster's sitting-room. Just Rebecca, a bit tired, a bit thinner, and a young bloke who couldn't be blamed for fancying your daughter, who came, if you only admitted it to yourself, in peace.

And over the meal you'd have felt quite different, too. You'd hardly have noticed the lack of meat, the surfeit of undercooked vegetables, that ghastly home-made herb-bread thing of Annie's that stuck to your palate when you tried to say something that might have lightened the atmosphere up a few notches. You wouldn't have needed the wine. You wouldn't even have mentioned the food at all, wouldn't have started that whole stupid conversation. Until last night you hadn't even known you felt like that about vegetarians. It wouldn't have occurred to you to try to draw someone out on the subject of battery chickens or veal-calves, or the digestive evils of red meat.

And the thing about his A-levels – how could you possibly have come out with something so transparent? Because what did it matter that he was brainy, what did it matter that he'd wiped the board in a way even Rebecca hadn't quite managed? It was no skin off your nose, surely? And you wouldn't normally have said any of that, all those meaningless compliments even he wasn't fooled by. And he wouldn't have blushed to the roots of his silly girlish hair. Rebecca wouldn't have given you that look. Jack and Izzie would just have gone on eating. Annie would have sat back in her chair, letting the talk drift over her, and smiled.

And then Annie would have slept with you as usual. She wouldn't have made that remark about the snoring. You would have gone straight up to your warm bed, and none of that messing about in the front room with sheets and pillows. None of that moving furniture around, late at night. You'd have been out of it. You wouldn't have noticed the full moon rising over the tiles, its white disc a

49

bit tarnished by the red haze of the streetlamps but still gleaming, still hanging there anyway. You wouldn't have heard the dustbin being kicked over at the end of the Fletchers' party, or the cats.

You would have fallen into deep sleep, in spite of everything. Nothing would have mattered. The meal wouldn't have lain on your gut like setting concrete. And when Izzie wandered in in the early, still-dark hours of the morning, you would have dealt with it properly. You would have heard what she had to say quickly, telling her it was only a dream, it wasn't anything. You would have taken her gently but firmly by the hand and led her back to her own bedroom. You would have turned on the light and looked down by the wall for her old Furry. You would have tucked her up tightly in her own bed.

And today would have had a quite different complexion to it. You wouldn't have given a damn that they weren't up, even at eleven. What did you care if they didn't show their faces till the evening? Annie would have made a pot of tea, and cooked you an egg. She would have cooked you *two* eggs. And when you went upstairs again to the bathroom you wouldn't even have noticed the door to the spare bedroom standing open and his bed empty, his shoes and jeans and Rebecca's grey fleece strewn right across the floor.

And when Rebecca finally appeared, still sleepy in her crumpled T-shirt, you would have been more careful. You would have stuck to plane-crashes or party politics or the weather. You wouldn't have noticed the way her hand shook as she filled the kettle, you wouldn't have picked off that long pale hair clinging to her shoulder. She wouldn't have looked at you. And you wouldn't have said anything, none of it, not a word, nothing. And if you'd only kept your mouth shut, you wouldn't be feeling any of what you're feeling now.

And perhaps then they would have stayed, the two of them, as they'd planned to originally. They'd still be here tonight. You'd have had a second chance. And if you and Ben had only started talking properly, you might have got under the cut-glass accent, you might have found you did have something in common after all, something you could both enjoy talking about when the women weren't around to spoil it. He might have had a sense of humour. He might have been good for Becky, even. He might have come here with you, left Beck with Annie to natter and come out to the pub with you like some young bloke at work you were quite matey with. You could have stood him a couple of pints.

And then they'd both still be around. None of that fuss about leaving, their bags cluttering the hall again, the dirty clothes bundled in all anyhow and crammed into the boot, the car doors slamming. Jack shrugging it all off and going back into his room, that deafening blast of music down the stairs. And Izzie like a waif at the top, looking down at you with big eyes.

And the business with Annie would never have happened. You might have stood at the open door smiling. From inside the car, Rebecca would have grinned back at you, waving at you frantically, still laughing and blowing kisses right up until the moment when Ben turned out into the main road. Annie would have leaned her head against your neck and sighed. You would have turned round and held her tightly, feeling her breasts and belly against your own body. And none of it need have been spoken. There wouldn't have been any call for any of it. Jack wouldn't have appeared in his doorway, glaring at you accusingly. And Izzie wouldn't have started that awful screaming. Izzie wouldn't have thrown herself downstairs and clung to Annie like that, beating you off as if you were some kind of animal. Jack wouldn't have gone back into his room and slammed the door.

And you wouldn't be here now. You wouldn't be sitting on your own like this next to that fucking one-armed bandit, or whatever they called them nowadays, you wouldn't be seeing all those little lights flash on and off in the corner of your eye. You wouldn't catch yourself half-following the pattern, half-watching a snake of little illuminated gold spots coil itself around the fascia of the machine, chasing its tail. You wouldn't be hearing that pounding bass from the jukebox, or watching the young kids with their tattoos, the regrowth of stubble on their bald heads. If you'd had time to think about it you could have done it quite differently. You could have brought Ben to this place straight away, the two of you quite impervious, sitting at the same small table, getting to know each other properly over a couple of beers, and no need for the whisky chasers. Becky at home with her mother. You could have got off on the right foot for once, been friendly and ordinary, two blokes together. Got rid of that little sarcastic something at the back of your throat and lived it all differently – that first meeting, the meal, this whole abortive weekend. That whole screwed-up thing with Jack and the girls. The waste with Annie. Those endless hours of sitting with the remote, flipping from channel to channel with the sound on mute.

The First Weekend

Rachel was driving, eighty in the fast lane, too close to the car in front, gesticulating with one hand as she spoke. She broke off suddenly. 'What the fuck was that?' she said.

Rob turned round and looked back. Behind them the cars were flashing their lights.

'Well? What do you think it was?' she was asking him again.

It was still early and the green slope of the Downs gleamed through a film of mist. For the moment the traffic was light. They drove on another few miles without speaking. Then he said, 'Can you pull off here?'

They swerved. 'I'm sorry, I'm...'

'It's all right,' he said. 'I just want to have a look at the car.'

'Why? What's the matter with the car?'

She slowed, following the exit slip-road. In the car-park he got out and walked round to the front. Rachel was watching him through the windscreen. There was no sign of any damage to the bonnet or the front bumper. Everything looked normal. No one was running after them, shouting or waving their arms. He said, 'I can't see anything.'

'I never touched it, Rob. You saw me. I wasn't anywhere near! You see something coming like that and it looks close, but actually it was a good three feet away.'

'All the same,' he said.

She took her hands off the wheel and buried her face in them. For a while he thought she might be crying. But when she finally looked up she only seemed tired.

Later, when they stopped for lunch, he forced himself to look at ordinary things – the overflowing bin-bags in their holders, that man over there in an anorak, huddled over his bunch of keys. 'Do you want to drive the next bit?' Rachel was asking him. She swept the crumbs on her lap out through the open door. She collected the rubbish up carefully and stuffed it into the glove-compartment. 'And I know it isn't easy for you. I know it does matter to you really. It's just that we never do much, as a family. Other people go out together. They have fun together. They do interesting things.'

It was hot in the car. He took off his jacket and threw it into the back. He rolled up his sleeves. 'Who are these other people? Where do they all go?'

Rachel was looking at him oddly. 'For God's sake, Rob!' She fastened her seat belt with a loud click.

The traffic on the motorway was heavier now. Abreast of him a lorry seemed to hang motionless in a cloud of noise and exhaust before inching ahead. He pulled into the slow lane behind it. 'We do spend time together. I take him swimming. I take him to matches sometimes.'

Rachel grunted. 'We hardly ever do anything together, the three of us.'

The tone of her voice made him take his eyes from the road for a moment to look at her. 'It was your idea to leave him this weekend.'

'I know.'

Ahead, the traffic was bunching, slowing for some kind of obstacle. He put his foot on the brake. A few yards ahead of them a huge articulated truck had pulled out to overtake. Behind it the cars queued, at dangerously short intervals. And he was trapped in the slow lane now. He'd have to wait until every last thing had gone past. 'It'll be good to see Pete and Steph, anyway,' he said.

She'd turned her face away from him and wound down the window slightly. Out of the corner of his eye he saw a strand of her hair lift and blow towards the crack. She turned back to him and put her hand on his thigh. 'What do you think it was?'

'What?'

'In the road, earlier. The thing we saw.'

Ahead of them, the fast lane was clear at last. He put his foot down. 'What did you think it was?'

She coughed. 'At first I thought it was a dummy. Thrown off the back of something, you know?'

He knew.

'And then I thought no, this is a real body. This is what a body would look like.'

He consciously relaxed his hands on the wheel.

After a while she said something else, the words so quiet he could hardly catch them. 'Should we have done something? Do you think we should have stopped?' Out of the corner of his eye he saw her lean towards him. 'He might not even have been dead.'

He replayed it in his mind, the flash of white face, the flap of something blue. 'He was dead,' he told her. Through his trousers he could feel her hand shaking. He took his own left hand from the wheel and put it over hers.

'How awful for you,' Steph said. 'What a good thing you were on your own!'

'You're right.' Rachel pushed a hand up into her hair. 'I never even...'

Rob put his arm round her shoulders. 'It's all right. He's asleep. I rang Mum. She read him a story and he didn't even ask about us. Stop worrying. He's fast asleep.'

Steph was stacking the plates and cutlery into the dishwasher. As she leaned forwards her top rode up slightly around her waist, baring a few inches of skin. The room came and went, the smell of coffee and snuffed candles, the white bar of light over the sink, the chink of dish against spoon. They moved into the lounge and he let his breath out slowly. It was a cool room with a pale carpet, uncluttered. Steph's design books were neatly stacked on a desk in one corner. Rachel went over to them and started leafing through the pages. Pete moved a pair of headphones from the seat of a chair and she jumped at the small noise. 'Your house is so wonderfully tidy!' she said.

'Not for much longer.' Pete laughed.

'Oh?' Rachel looked at Steph. 'Are you...?'

'Steph's finally starting her own business,' Pete said. 'The loan came through a few days ago. She's going into it with a friend. They're just looking for some suitable premises.' He frowned slightly. 'She's not actually going to run it from home. But you know what she's like, how obsessive she gets once she starts in on something. And then she's going to tell me she's exhausted. It's not going to be the same.'

'Is that right, Steph?' He found himself watching her as she came in carefully, carrying a tray. She closed the door behind her with a little movement of her bum and set the tray down on the table. When she reached forward her top clung to her back and shoulders, showing the knobs of her spine.

She turned suddenly and grinned. 'It's my business, Rob. I don't know why he's so steamed up about it. It's got nothing to do with him.'

In the kitchen the light was still on. The dishwasher hummed gently. He poured himself a second cup of coffee and stood drinking it at the sink, staring out into the darkness on the other side of the glass. His own face was superimposed on it, white above the collar of his blue shirt. For a moment he saw the body again, a fleeting impression of dark blue clothing and something paler. He put down his cup on the draining-board and went outside.

He could smell grass and trees, the faint prickle of smoke from somewhere. He took a deep breath, opening his mouth wide, and started to yawn. His eyes streamed with tears. It was like when Will yawned. He'd start and not be able to stop sometimes. 'You are tired, Father William,' Rachel would say, with mock firmness, and whisk him off to bed. He saw himself and Will as they'd been in the back garden last Sunday, Will prodding the ground with the cricket-bat that was too big for him, screwing up his eyes against the sun. Rob had stood behind him and put his arms round him to show him the right position. He remembered the feel of Will's small body inside his arms, the way he wriggled and looked backwards up at him and laughed, the brush of his son's hair on his cheek. And then Rachel had called them both in for tea. Will had turned to him and made a face. But they'd gone in anyway, and washed their hands. After tea they'd sneaked out again and played on into dusk, throwing and swooping and diving, until the ball was practically invisible against the dark grass.

'I know what you mean,' he said. They were driving back towards the east, the sun setting in the rear-view mirror. 'I kept seeing it too.'

'Just those few seconds as we shot past.' Rachel bent down. She was undoing her shoelaces. 'All weekend I kept seeing it over and over again.'

'It's something the brain does,' he said. 'It's how the brain deals with shock.'

'That syndrome.' Rachel put one bare foot up against the dashboard, her toenails little red splashes against the grey. 'Post-traumatic. It's the way the mind's supposed to heal itself.'

They were getting quite near the place. For a few minutes he drove without speaking. Rachel reached out and turned the knob on the radio and music burst out suddenly. The Beatles, something about hiding your head in the sand, something before their time. He turned down the volume.

Rachel said suddenly, 'I've realised what it must have been.'

'What?'

'An accident.'

He pulled out to overtake a caravan. He glanced at the driver of the car as he passed. A man, elderly, with grey hair and glasses. He said carefully, 'I did get a sort of impression that the cars on the other carriageway had stopped.' He could feel her turn to look at him. The radio was hardly more than a whisper of tinny treble. He reached out and turned it off. 'I wonder if Will'll be glad to see us.'

Rachel laughed suddenly. 'Knowing your Mum, she'll have spoilt him rotten. I bet he'll be cross with us for coming back so soon!'

This was the place. They were going more slowly than they had been then. He had time to get a good look. But there was no broken glass, no stains on the road, nothing that looked like burnt rubber or blood. He began to relax.

Ahead of him, towards Kent, the traffic was thinning. 'I'll put him to bed tonight, if you like.'

She wasn't listening. He took his eyes from the road briefly to glance at her. She had her hands over her face again. When she took them away she swivelled in the seatbelt and drew her legs up on to the seat. 'Rob?'

'Yes?'

'The body...' Her voice caught and she stopped suddenly.

He took a deep breath. 'The body,' he said.

'It looked weird.'

What did she expect him to say?

He could feel her looking at him, leaning forward towards him in her seat. She said, 'I keep seeing it. All weekend. There was something funny about it.'

The traffic would be dividing in a minute. He needed to be in the right-hand lane. He checked his mirrors and eased across.

'All weekend I've kept thinking...'

The broken white line thickened to a white train-track and he leaned back in his seat, pressing his spine hard into the upholstery.

'I... It was the head. It looked so big. Out of proportion – like a child's almost. For a while I thought perhaps it was a child. Then I thought no, there was something wrong with it. It was swollen, or something.'

He pushed his back into the seat and took a deep breath as the lanes divided, then swung left on to the sliproad for the A21.

'And then I started to wonder if it wasn't the head. Perhaps it was the body that wasn't right. Maybe it wasn't… whole.'

They were climbing a steep hill. He had to speak loudly to make himself heard over the engine. 'It definitely wasn't a whole body.' He felt himself shouting. 'It was just the top half of a body. It was cut off at the hip.' In the seat beside him he sensed Rachel move away, resting her head against the window. At the top of the hill a concrete bridge made a wide, airy curve against the pale sky and in a moment they were passing underneath. The Weald lay spread out in front of them, the river Medway glittering in the low sun. Then they were rushing down the other side towards Will, and Rachel's mother, their little house full of dirty laundry, cluttered with furniture and toys.

Upstairs

Afterwards she could never quite remember if she had actually seen anything fall past the window. She must have been sitting at her drawing-board as usual, a thin brush between her fingers. She had almost certainly been drawing a red line round the edges of a piece of land. The line would have bulged suddenly where something had made her jump – an egg travelling down the neck of a red snake.

Or perhaps she hadn't seen it at all. Perhaps she'd only heard the noises, the voices rising from the asphalt forecourt, the siren of the ambulance as it turned in from the main road. Behind her the other plans assistants pushed back their chairs and crowded towards the glass. She stood up and went to join them. But it was impossible to make out anything – only a milling group of heads, the red flash of a blanket, metal doors standing open, everything blinking in the rotating light. Around her, the room was suddenly almost empty. She felt Stephen's hand in hers, pulling her out into the corridor and down the stairs, into the edges of the crowd. *'What...?'* *'Who....?'* Suddenly she was shivering. She realised she knew without asking who the dead girl was.

She'd spoken to her only once. It was when they were both new, both in Training Group. As she'd reached to push open the fire-doors at the end of the corridor they'd opened towards her, making her step back suddenly. The water in her jam-jar had slopped over on to her cuff. 'You fool,' she'd said.

'Sorry. I didn't see you.' The girl coming the other way coloured slightly and looked down at her feet.

'It's all right. No damage done.' Flat, boat-like shoes, baggy cardigan, hairslide slipping down over one eye. 'Don't I know you?' The words echoed on the cement surfaces of the building. 'Haven't we seen each other somewhere before?'

'Ruth Inglis,' the girl said quickly. 'We were at school together. You wouldn't remember me. You were a year ahead.'

'But...?'

'We did Spanish together.'

'Oh. Right.'

The girl eased herself through the doors and let them swing gently shut behind her. She looked up with a shy smile. 'Who would've thought either of us'd end up in a place like this?'

'Yeah,' Jo said. She was starting to blush too. 'Well, at least here it isn't irregular verbs. At least we're getting paid for it. I can't say I lie awake at night thinking, "Oh, God, I've missed my vocation!" '

'Don't you?' The girl, Ruth, had stopped smiling.

'It's fine actually,' Jo said. 'You'll enjoy it. Most of the time it's a bit of a laugh. There're some really nice people.'

Ruth was looking down at her shoes again, biting the inside of her cheek. Jo remembered thinking, *Oh, fuck it*, pushing hard with the flat of her hand against the graph-paper glass of the door.

After a while they stopped watching and went back to their drawing-boards. Over towards the north-east the sky had gone cloudy and the room was darker than usual. The desk-lamps came on one by one. In the far corner someone laughed. Somewhere just behind her she heard someone whisper, 'But why would she...?' She closed her ears. It was pointless even to ask. When did you ever know what made people do things in life? She glanced across the top of her drawing-board at Stephen, trying to catch his eye, but he seemed determined not to look up. She slipped quietly down from her chair and out of the room.

The crowds had gone now. Everyone else was working. The ambulance would be miles away already, on some other errand. The policemen would be cruising the town centre in their patrol-car, bored, turning to each other to crack a joke. Where the body had lain there was a white chalk outline. A kind of ghost still lay here, traced on the asphalt – its limbs fatter and stubbier than Ruth's had been. Jo leaned closer to the glass. It was hard to believe they really did that – outlined a fallen body in chalk. As if a white shape could tell you what it was someone had been thinking, what it was that made someone decide to jump. When all it was really was a piece of tarmac with a line round it, a shape that could mean almost anything. When work ended at five-thirty, hundreds of people would stream past. Some of them wouldn't even notice. One or two would step right into the space between the chalked lines and feel a friendly hand yanking them sideways and laugh with embarrassment.

As she slid back into her seat Stephen finally looked up. He bent to open his drawer and threw something at her without warning. She caught it by reflex. An apple, wrapped in a piece of paper. She put it down on the desk and it rolled under the drawing-board, out of sight. She smoothed out the crumpled note. 'Come down to Sussex with me for the weekend?' Opposite her he was eating an apple of his own, munching steadily as he drew. She stared absently out of the window, over the jumble of lower buildings. From here she could pick out the flaking roof of the Training Group hut. Inside, they'd be mixing colour-washes and exchanging jokes. She measured the sprawl of the car-park, its multi-coloured rows of cars. And beyond the site boundaries, the treetops, the irregular brick and slate surfaces of the town. She took a deep breath, picked up her fine pen and dipped it into blue ink; wrote '*Chez Nous*' on the plan in italic script, beside the neat little square of a house. Then another: '*Rhododendrons*'. She dipped her nib, her hand still shaking. The shaft of the pen rattled against the glass.

In Training Group they'd all been new to it – all, in a sense, kids. They were Fred's kids. They'd giggled, jogging one another's elbows as they carried their jam-jars of pink water to the toilets to wash them out. They'd swapped stories as they rinsed their brushes under the cold tap and walked back along the cement corridors of the Nissen hut to the big, light room they all shared. They'd exchanged erasers and tracing-paper and Indian ink. They'd egged one another on to trace off the perfect plan, the black inked lines clear and true, the corners just meeting, without the slightest suspicion of a gap or an overlap, so perfect it might have been produced by a machine. As each of them mastered the technique, Fred would enter a little tick in his book, next to the person's name. She practised the blue and pink washes until the colours were completely uniform, not a blotch or a pooling of pigment anywhere, not a single stray dark hair from the head of the brush. The room was still and silent around her as she drew out a long narrow band of carmine round the four edges of a single designated plot.

And if there'd been some sort of award for application and neatness, she'd surely have won it: at the end of the six weeks she could outline a property without the slightest tremor. 'Good girl!' Fred had been standing at her shoulder. She hadn't even noticed him. Her ultramarine italics might have been printed, they were so small and regular. '*Chez Nous*,' she'd written, for practice. '*Shangri-la.*' '*Little Pippins.*' And in black, perfectly regular capitals, 'WESTLAKE ROAD', 'MONTPELIER AVENUE', 'CHESTNUT CLOSE'.

One afternoon near the end of her training, Fred had called her over, a battered pink file in his hands. 'Jo, can you take this up to room 614?' He waved the file in her face. 'Give it to the officer in charge, will you, sweetheart? And have a good look round while you're up there, eh? Check it out. You'll be up there yourself Monday.'

'Monday?'

He mimicked her expression, pursing his mouth, making big eyes. 'Come on, love, what did you expect? You can't stay down here for ever. We all have to move on upstairs eventually.'

She didn't trust herself to answer. She stood there and stretched out her hand. She walked over to the main building. She went in by the big front entrance and took the side door to the stairs. Six floors. Her feet sounded on the concrete steps, echoing in the stairwell, following her to the top. On the sixth floor landing she paused for a moment to get her breath. She stood there for a couple of minutes with her forehead pressed against the glass.

Room 614 was a big room, double the length of the others, full of high desks, the far wall all windows, an almost blinding expanse. Between the drawing-boards, green plants twined around the stems of angle-poise lamps. The supervisor sat on his own at a lower table, in the corner farthest from the door. She went up to him and handed him the pink file. 'I've brought this from Fred Cooper.' He hardly glanced at her as his stubby fingers untied the tape and felt inside for the sheaf of documents. He flipped through the pages to find the original. She waited as he made a jotted note in pencil on a pad in front of him. She watched him fold the deeds up again in their original creases and slide them back inside the cardboard envelope.

He knotted the tape again clumsily and laid the file down on his desk. Then he folded his arms and looked up at her. 'So we'll be seeing you up here on Monday, will we?' He gestured with his head towards an empty drawing-board at the far end. 'If you'd like to bring your things up tomorrow after lunch, move yourself in. Then you can start straight away, without a lot of messing about.' He picked the file up and lobbed it in among some others that were waiting for attention in a bin.

She nodded and made for the door, past the desk that must be her own, the only unclaimed space in a jungle of gourd- and spider-plants. Her eyes met the eyes of the boy opposite. His smile stayed with her as she turned right along the corridor and made for the fire-door to the stairwell at the end.

The trees looked gold now, lit by the afternoon sun, the roads between them blocked out precisely in light and shadow, each house in its own little area of garden. You could see the boundaries so clearly it was almost like looking at a plan.

She wanted the journey down to Sussex to go on for ever – Stephen's thigh against her thigh, and the rocking of the train. Outside, fields that opened and closed in a fan. The high cables that seemed to want to lift off from the earth rose and fell in the sky as she watched them. She could go on like this for days and nights, pretending to be completely absorbed in the landscape, not moving even an inch in case she broke the spell. For years even, the edges of her body against his, till the train finally slowed and drew in under the dirty glass.

When they stepped out on to the platform, there were gulls screaming. At first she wasn't sure where the noise was coming from. She licked her lips, and tasted salt. Somewhere outside the station she heard an ambulance siren slide from one note to the next as it went by.

At the door his mother opened her arms. Stephen stepped forward into the hall and let himself be hugged. She hung back, under the dark overhang of the porch. When they'd finished his mother turned to her. 'You must be Jo.'

The house was small and cramped. The narrow passage led back into the kitchen and the bathroom, separated by a kind of airlock. A door to one side opened on a tiny space crowded with furniture. It was difficult to walk to the sofa without banging your knees on the coffee table and chairs. It was a relief to be offered tea, to sit quietly with the cup and saucer balanced on her lap. On the sofa, Stephen's mother sat next to her son. She looked at Jo as she put her arm round him and gave him a squeeze. 'You don't mind me doing this, do you, Jo?' She was laughing. 'I don't see much of him, now he's got this wonderful new job. And I miss him. Wait till you have children, you'll see what I mean.' Stephen was looking down. He picked off a piece of light cotton that had stuck to the nap of his cords and sat with it in his hand, rolling it backwards and forwards between his finger and thumb. 'Come here,' his mother said. She stretched out her hand for the little ball of grey fluff, laughing when he deposited it obediently in her palm.

Jo found herself banished to the tiny spare bedroom over the stairs. There were frilly curtains, and dried flowers in a china vase on the mantelpiece. She prized open the stiff drawers of the dressing-table and discovered female underclothes, sweaters wrapped in clear plastic, lavender-bags disintegrating in a mess of little grains. For a moment she took them for larvae or eggs and almost cried out.

The sheets smelled as if they hadn't been slept in for months. She pulled them up to her chin and waited for the crack of light under the door to go out. When everything went black she lay without moving for perhaps half an hour. Then she slid out from under the blankets and tiptoed across the floor to where the pencil of light had been. She turned the handle quietly and stood listening. In the faint glow from a streetlamp two houses down she could just make out the outline of the door to Stephen's room. From where she stood it was only a matter of a few feet. In the darkness she could almost feel him waiting. Behind the other door at the end of the passageway she heard a dry crack, the sound of someone turning over in bed. She crept back to her own. The stiff covers gradually moulded themselves to her body, pressing down on her limbs, squeezing breath from her lungs as if she'd fallen from a great height.

The next day, when they got back, the little front room was full of people. There was no way the two of them could slip past. Inside, a little man sat on the piano-stool, one of his trouser-legs hiked up slightly as he scratched at the ribbing of his sock. A younger, slightly plumper version of Stephen's mother patted the cushion beside her own. Stephen went over and sat down next to her on the couch. She was looking from him to Jo and back again. 'So did you have a good walk, you two?' She glanced at Jo and her mouth pursed up slightly. 'How's our golden boy, then?' Jo saw her reach across to touch Stephen's hair. He ducked away from her, laughing. 'Was it blowy enough for you out there? What did you get up to?'

Stephen didn't answer. He stood up and went out, towards the kitchen. Jo heard the sound of water running, the rising note of the kettle as he filled it. His aunt turned back to her and shrugged. 'And what do you do, Jo?'

'Oh, me...' Jo said. 'I... ' Around her the room had gone suddenly quiet. They were all listening to her, waiting for her to answer. 'I'm a Plans Assistant.'

'That sounds interesting. Do you enjoy it?'

'Oh, yes.' She heard herself laugh nervously. 'Well, I'm still there, so I suppose I must.'

'What is it you do exactly? What does the job involve?' It was the man's voice. He shot the question at her, half-scowling. His bare ankle was exposed, resting on his other knee, the skin at the top of the sock red with scratch-marks.

'Do?'

'What do you do? What does being a Plans Assistant consist of?'

They were all listening to her intently. The man, the aunt, Stephen's mother. In the open doorway, Stephen himself, standing with a box of tea-bags in his hand. 'Come on, Jo. Tell them.' Even Stephen was expecting her to say something tactful and polite.

'It doesn't consist of anything much.' Her voice was shaking suddenly with anger. 'You draw a red line round a piece of land on a map.'

The man on the stool grunted. 'Why would you want to do that?'

'To show where the boundaries are.'

Stephen's aunt was leaning towards her now. 'And that's it?'

'Yes.'

She uncrossed her legs. On the narrow mantelpiece the clock ticked.

'All day? You just sit there all day drawing a red line?'

She was trying to stop herself from shouting at him, her face aching from the effort of holding itself still. 'That's it,' she said. 'Well, more or less.'

'I'm surprised you like it then,' his aunt said. 'I'd have thought that might get a bit boring.'

'It does,' Jo said. 'Actually it's excruciating. It's a dead-end job, for complete morons. I'm going to hand in my notice any day now.'

For a moment no one said anything. The uncle shifted on his stool. 'And you're a Plans Assistant, you say?' He turned to Stephen's mother. 'But Maggie, isn't that what…? Steve? Isn't that…?'

Jo heard Stephen shout something over the noise of the kettle. She looked up to see him standing in the doorway again, his face damp with steam. 'She's right,' he said. 'We draw lines round things. Pretty exciting, huh?' Then he was gone. She heard the whistle rise to a long shriek before dying away.

On the journey back they sat as far away from each other as they could, in opposite corners of the compartment. After a while Steve stood up and went out into the corridor, the landscape from the opposite window rushing across the dark cloth of his back. Jo turned her face away. The brown fields were dotted with gulls, following them inland. The ruts were full of water, and the water was silver from the sky. No people anywhere. Just the telegraph-poles, at regular intervals along the track, their cat's-cradle of wire rising and falling. Watching the poles flick past was like watching another moving train: after a while something happened to your eyes or your brain and you seemed to see them going the wrong way. She felt the blood rush to her face as she remembered the little front room with its kindly upturned faces. She saw Steve's involuntary grimace as his mother's arm squeezed his shoulders. She tried to concentrate, to recapture that fraction of a second of darkness, like the flap of a bird's wing, as the girl's body fell. On the other side of the glass the telegraph wires were trying to float upwards, towards a silver-grey gleam of evening sky as the train travelled north. They'd be almost making it and then another pole would come.

Heavy

There's no law that says that the night before your brother's funeral everyone in the whole world has to be friendly. All the same, it can take some getting used to. When the four of us walked into the Heather Bar in Moss End, they saw at once we were English. They stopped watching the T.V. screen for a moment and turned round to watch us as we trooped past, following us with their eyes.

We found an empty alcove in the back room and sat down, behind the glass partition. I put my hands flat on the table, then pushed myself up. 'Well? What's everyone having?' No matter what I did, my voice sounded unreal here – I never lived in the area long enough to pick up the accent. 'What'll you have?' I asked them all again.

Ros leaned against me for a moment, her hair catching slightly on my cheek. We'd left home early and I hadn't had time to shave. She straightened up and blinked. 'Whisky,' she said. 'That's what they drink here, isn't it?' Her face in the lights was an odd colour, grey almost. My own hands were shaking. We all needed something fast. I looked at Jim and Nicky, but they still seemed dazed, dithering. So I stood up and went to the bar. 'Two whiskies, two pints of heavy,' I said.

Around me they'd all stopped talking. The barman served me without speaking. From the T.V. mounted on the wall in the corner by the door there were shouts, a gust of cheering; the crowd was singing something familiar. 'Who's playing?' I could see it was England, but the other team could have been out of Mars. Over the last few weeks I'd completely lost track.

'Argentina.' One of the drinkers gestured towards the screen. 'And England.' Said with a kind of derisive jerk.

'What's the score?'

'Two all. In extra time.'

'I'm sorry?'

'Extra time!' He took a swig from his pint glass and banged it down again on the bar.

I picked up the two pints and carried them back to the table, froth running down over my fingers. I went back for the whiskies and gave them to Nicky and Ros. Back here behind the partition it wasn't so loud. You could hear yourself think, anyway. I raised my glass. 'To Paddy,' I said.

'He would have enjoyed this,' Ros said. 'It's his kind of place.' She reached over and put her hand on top of mine.

'He could talk the language.' Nicky smiled faintly.

'Do you remember, Mike, when we were little...' Jim started. He tailed off, staring at the wall.

Ros said to me quickly, 'I remember when I first knew you. He must have been about ten. I can still see him lying on the floor with that book of football stickers. He was so...'

But she couldn't finish either. Nicky changed the subject quickly and for a while we just drank and talked about other things. Then I let my eyes be pulled back to the T.V. screen, flashing grass-green and purple through the partition. The end of extra time, and still a draw by the look of it. The men on the other side were leaning back, their elbows on the bar. They were grinning, exchanging short remarks. I found I was mentally crossing my fingers for England. I emptied my glass. Someone else roared something to someone across the room.

'Tomorrow morning...' Jim started. 'How are we...?'

'In the car,' I said. 'There's plenty of room for all of us. Don't worry. It'll be all right.'

Ros was shivering.

'Are you cold?' I asked her. But she took another mouthful of whisky and shook her head. We all looked up as an odd sound went up in the other room – half cheer, half groan. 'Looks like time's run out,' I said.

Nicky turned round in her seat so that her back was towards the glass. 'I can't watch.'

'You don't need to watch.' Jim gave a short laugh.

On the screen a white blur moved across the grass and sent the ball spinning into the back of the net. The netting shook. They showed it again in slow motion and it shook more slowly, the man moved back and punched the air with a kind of grace, his hair lifting like in a shampoo advert. They showed it again, from another angle. The men in the other bar were quiet, watching grimly. Then the Argentinian moved up and pounded the ball into the goal-mouth, and a great cheer went up. I caught a snatch of 'Don't Cry for Me, Argentina'. That must have been what they'd been singing earlier. Someone else was getting a fresh round. I drained my glass and pushed it away from me. 'What did he ever do to deserve this?' I said.

'Nothing.' Nicky wiped her mouth with the back of her hand. 'He didn't do anything. He was an ordinary bloke, with an ordinary job. He never did anything to hurt anyone. But he wasn't frightened, either. He stayed.'

'We didn't know him, not really,' Jim said. 'Our little brother, and we didn't ever really even...'

'Can we talk about something else?' Ros's voice was muffled. She was speaking through her hands. She took them away and looked up. 'I'm sorry.' She blinked quickly and turned her head away.

'We're all sorry.' The beer had left spidery trails of wet on the table. I moved my glass across and they ran together, shining purple, then green. Behind me the outer bar was suddenly filled with cheering, and I knew England had missed.

'He would've hated this part, anyway.' Nicky made a face.

'He would've cared, and not cared,' I told her. 'He would've minded England losing. But he wouldn't't've given a fuck what anyone else thought.'

Behind us the cheering had risen to a frenzy. I didn't have to look round to know what they were doing. They'd joined arms in a sort of dance, pounding the floor. 'We're going home...' The words of the song were just comprehensible. Then, 'Don't cry for me' again. The circle surged and swayed, the faces glistening with sweat and triumph, the slurred voices louder and louder. Every so often one of them would look over in our direction with something like a smirk. 'The truth is...'

Our glasses were empty. We stood up, scraping our chair-legs on the floor, and made our way through the outer bar. The women went first, heads down, Ros with her hands in her pockets. Then Jim, not looking up, not meeting anyone's eyes. Easing our way between the damp, jigging bodies. I raised my head just once, to glance at a man near the open door. He was sagging visibly, his shirt unbuttoned halfway down his chest. Our eyes met, his vague and unfocused. 'Sae ye didna win this teem, reet?' he said, making a thumbs up sign with his left hand. He went to take a swig from his glass but it seemed to be empty. He turned it upside-down and a thin dribble ran down on to the floor. 'Nae hard feelens?'

I could have shown him how hard my feelings were. He would have sat down suddenly in a puddle, wondering what'd come at him. But I didn't. I stepped out on to the pavement. I blinked at the ten o'clock twilight. *The truth is, we're going home.* And Paddy chose to stay.

We huddled together in our pew at the front. A modern building, kite-shaped, tapering to a point behind the altar at the East end. No windows you could see out of. Just a smooth expanse of stone floor and polished wood, a platform where the altar was, and the coffin in the central aisle in front of it, shining. There was a smell which must be coming from the lilies in the big set-pieces on either side, or from the choir women over on our left.

There were so many of them. Not just the singers, but other people, too – old friends of Mum's and Dad's, friends and colleagues of Paddy's we hadn't had the faintest idea about. The whole place seemed full of them. Well-wishers, presumably – they'd hardly come to heckle or scratch the backs of the pews with graffiti, not at a funeral, anyway. We kept our heads down, not meeting their eyes. I concentrated on standing up when they stood up. I sat or knelt down when they sat or knelt.

And it was okay. The Mass rolling on steadily and all of us rising slowly with it like commuters on an escalator, eyes absently following the ads as they went past. It didn't touch me, any of it, not really. Too long ago now, all that – since I was an altar boy at St Barnabas, worrying about whether anyone'd notice my shoes under the cassock, or whether I'd get to be the one to put the candles out. There wasn't anything to be nervous of, when it came down to it – nothing that might have struck a chord, or reminded me. My lungs filled and emptied themselves again, over and over. After a while I found I didn't even have to think about it. It wasn't going to be that bad. I'd been in danger of taking it all too seriously, as Mum used to say. I could hear her voice telling me, the mumbly Cork accent. I could see her exchange a sideways look with Paddy and laugh.

There was a shuffling as everyone sat down. In my lap my hands were clenched together. I relaxed my fingers and pulled them apart, then joined them again more loosely. By the time I looked up, the priest was already standing at the lectern in his white robes.

It took my breath away, he was so young. Good-looking, hair cropped so close to his head he looked like any young kid you'd pass on Sauchiehall Street or on a station platform, barely more than twenty. And when he spoke I could hear straight away that he was a local boy, someone from around here, no trace of the Irish accent I'd been expecting – a west coast voice but muted, not so hard to understand, and under the voice itself something else, not the usual bland all-purpose sing-song but something gruffer and younger, altogether harder to place. He might have been trying not to cry.

'You may be thinking...' he started. 'You may be wondering why I'm wearing these robes.' A slight colour had come to his cheeks. His pale eyes seemed to go milky behind the lenses of the round, wire-rimmed glasses. 'They're not funeral robes, I hear you saying to yourselves... And you'd be correct. They're *not* funeral robes. They're ordination robes. In fact they're the robes I wore to my own ordination just this last week. Paddy...' His voice seemed to catch on the name and he looked down, then quickly back at us. 'Patrick was a member of the choir of this church. And as a member of the choir of this church...' I glanced at Ros beside me in the pew, but all I could see was her profile, determinedly expressionless. Under her eyelid something glinted, but she didn't blink. The young priest cleared his throat, and started again, his voice louder and more confident now, reaching right to the very back. 'As a member of the choir of this church, Patrick came here regularly every week to practise the special music that was to be sung on that occasion. He came every week, whatever the weather, whatever other demands he may have had on his time. As far as I'm aware he'd not missed a single rehearsal. Even the last.' He paused for a moment. In the block of pews on the other side of the aisle the choir seemed to be swallowing, clearing its collective throat. A sheaf of music fell to the floor with a quiet hiss.

'We all hoped he'd be here on the day.' He looked down at his shoes, black and polished on the pale flooring. 'And in a way he was. I can assure you...' He raised his head to look straight at me and I felt my throat constrict suddenly. '...that though Paddy wasn't in fact able to be here on that occasion, there wasn't a single one of us who didn't think of him with affection and miss the sound of his voice.' Beside me Ros had broken down, crying silently, her shoulders shaking. From behind me I heard Nicky sniff loudly and Jim change his weight from foot to foot. 'As it happens, this is my first funeral.' The young voice was stronger than ever now, a boy forgetting himself. 'So it seemed right and appropriate to wear these white robes today in Paddy's memory, and for us all to sing some of that fine music he practised, in celebration...' The word rang out to the pale shell of the building. 'Not only in sadness, but also in celebration... of how and where he lived and what sort of person he was.'

There was another stirring as we sat down. My hands were clenching, unclenching, the polished wooden ledge in front of us reflecting a blur of movement, then still again. And then they were singing, the whole place echoing to their voices. And when it was finished the women in the choir pews were sobbing openly, their arms round one another in comfort, so that when it was finally time for Jim and me to step forward into the aisle and shoulder the coffin, I'd almost lost my sense of the oddness of it all, the stiff white folds of the flowers, the crowd of strangers in their dark anoraks and raincoats, the way Ros turned her head away as she stood up to let me squeeze past. The flame of the nearest candle wavered and sent out a sudden small jet of smoke that melted into nothing as it rose towards the ceiling. I hardly noticed how heavy or how light he was.

Back at the house, none of us knew quite what to do with ourselves. Somewhere inside my head I could still hear singing. The local people had gone off somewhere. They'd come up to us shyly and offered their condolences, and then gone off in little groups of four or five, until only the young priest was left. Then even he turned and went back up the steps and into the church.

What would Paddy have said to him? Would he have done more than just shake his hand? I sat on the arm of the sofa and looked out of the back window at an old bathtub lying in the long grass. It was half-full of rainwater, a rim of dark scum floating near the edges. A gust of wind caught it side-on and the surface of the water shuddered.

Nicky walked past me and stopped, bending her knees slightly to look into my face. She passed her hand backwards and forwards in front of my eyes. Then she stood up straight again and went into the kitchen. I could hear drawers being pulled out, cupboard doors banging, the clashing of metal pans, the soft suck of the rubber seal on the freezer as it was pulled apart.

She walked back in and stood in the middle of us, rubbing her hands. 'We're hungry, that's what it is. We must all be ravenous. The freezer's packed with stuff.'

Jim looked at her. 'You mean, you're thinking of using something?'

Nicky shrugged. 'I don't see why not. Fish and chips, chicken and chips, lasagne, whatever. You name it. It's probably in there. All we have to do is get it out and stick it in the oven. Say what you feel like, and I'll do it.'

'Actually, I don't think I feel very much like anything,' Jim said.

Ros pushed herself up from her armchair and slipped out. No one spoke. After about a minute I got up too and followed her upstairs.

*

The bathroom door was shut and locked. I wandered through the upstairs rooms, the two smaller bedrooms with their stacked furniture and threadbare carpets, the master bedroom that had been Paddy's. He'd painted it a deep wine colour. Across the dark ceiling, a spattering of white blobs that looked like popcorn or chewing-gum. A pale grey carpet that was soft under my feet when I took my shoes off. An old bureau. Shelves of CDs, tapes, books.

I opened the door to the cupboard, and stuck my head inside. It was big enough to walk into, if there had only been room to put my feet. But the whole thing was stuffed to bursting point – shelves of tins and boxes and papers in untidy stacks, files going back to his schooldays – I could see the Academy crest on one of them – exercise books, even. Clothes he'd been too busy or too lazy to throw out. And on the floor even more boxes, larger. I knelt down and pulled the nearest one towards me, out into the room.

It was full of football stuff – cards bunched together with rubber bands, dog-eared rosettes, a red and white scarf. I pulled one end of it and the rest followed, stretching, springing back towards me in a shower of crumbs and fluff and crumpled sweet-papers. I shook it out and wound it round my own neck.

In the bottom of the box there was a football. It was old and soft – it probably hadn't been pumped up for years. It felt heavy in my arms. I knelt on the bed and pushed the window wider. Then I threw the ball out into the back garden. It caught the edge of the bath and bounced out into the long grass at the foot of the silver birch. I closed my eyes, smelling Paddy through the scarf. In my mind's eye the ball was bouncing ever more slowly, in, out, in, out, in. Someone was punching the air, gracefully jumping in slow motion to throw himself at another player's neck.

'Mike?' I turned round to see Jim standing in the doorway. He looked at me, taking in the scarf. 'Mike, we ordered Chinese. Are you coming down? Nicky and Ros're just unpacking it now.'

'Are you all right?' Ros was undressing, laying her dark clothes neatly over the arm of a chair and shrugging on the oversized T-shirt she wore at night.

'I'm fine.'

She came and stood by me and held my hand, stroking it gently with her thumb. 'Sleep,' she said. Then, 'Don't worry about tomorrow. I'll drive the first couple of hundred, if you like.'

I shrugged. 'I'm not worried.' It was true. In one sense it was true. I pulled off my own clothes and got into bed. Ros was taking her lenses out. I could hear the tiny clink of the tablet against the side of the little plastic cup, the almost inaudible spurt of the solution. I lay looking up. It reminded me of a cinema, that plum-coloured ceiling, and the scattered grains of the popcorn, sticking exactly where people had thrown them, not falling back down.

She came over and got in beside me, the two of us squashed together in Paddy's single bed, all knees and elbows. 'Just like old times,' she said. 'Like in Southampton, do you remember?'

I lay tense, not letting myself relax against her. I was afraid she'd want to start something, and I wasn't sure I was in the mood for it. In fact, I was bloody sure I wasn't. But she didn't. She only said, 'Well, at least the World Cup'll be almost over by the time we get back.' She raised herself on one elbow to reach across me and turn out the bedside light.

And then we gasped, both of us together. The whole room seemed to catch its breath suddenly. Together we lay staring at the ceiling. 'Jesus!' she said.

Above us the darkness was alive with little points of light, brighter than anything you ever see through that pink haze you get everywhere now. I can't remember anything like it even when I was a kid, long before Dad even thought of moving up here. We were falling upwards into a deep bowl of stars. I fixed my eyes on one particular group. It seemed to be coming towards me, then it zoomed off again into the distance. 'He couldn't manage to do even that right,' I said.

Ros turned her face towards mine on the pillow. I could just make out the whites of her eyes. 'What do you mean?'

'He ought to have mapped them out properly, the real constellations.' In all that light-speckled expanse, there was nothing I recognised.

'No. Wait!' Ros had slipped out of bed. She'd picked up Paddy's old torch from the bedside table and was rifling hurriedly through the books. She got back in beside me, a big child's encyclopaedia in her hands. She sat turning the pages, screwing up her eyes against the glare. She found the illustration she wanted and angled the book so that I could see it too. 'Look!'

I looked. I couldn't see anything.

She turned the book round slowly and suddenly something inside my head clicked. That group there – it was the same. And that one. And all the others. The pattern on the page matched the pattern over our heads. 'There. Got it?'

'I think so.'

She read off the names, stumbling slightly over the small print: ' "Canis Major", "Dorado", "Triang Aust", "Crux…"' In the light of the torch she was looking at me. It was a question.

' "…Australis"?'

Next to my eyes, the soft bulk of the pillow scrunched itself into wrinkles. 'Why?' she said.

I shrugged and the quilt slipped, exposing my upper arm. I yanked it back into place, burrowing into her warm shoulder. She leaned away from me to close the book and put it down carefully on the bedside table. A couple of seconds later the torch went out. Over us I could sense the southern sky, brighter than ever. We lay there like spoons, her T-shirt rucked up to her waist, her arse warm in my lap. *The truth is.* In my mind's eye I could see Paddy at about thirteen, sprawled across the trailing bedclothes, a half-finished glass of Irn Bru on the bedside table, the glossy page of a football annual creasing under his cheek. He opened his eyes and grinned. For a moment I thought I could hear singing.

Mother-of-Pearl

When I unlock the door of the flat and walk in the first thing I see is my mum's face. She's been here all day, waiting. While I was at work, while I was shopping in my lunch hour, while I was on the tube coming home. Now she's standing here with my gran, the two of them shoulder to shoulder in the narrow hall.

I throw the plastic carrier-bag I'm holding through the bedroom doorway as I push past. My gran looks at it, and makes a sour face. My mum starts twisting her hands with excitement. I can see she's having to make a real effort. She can hardly stop herself from grabbing the carrier and ripping at the tissue paper to find out what's inside.

They follow me into the kitchen, watch me as I unplug the kettle and take it to the tap to fill it with fresh water. I can feel them standing just behind me. My gran says, 'Is that a kettle?' And then, 'What's it made of, bakelite?'

My mum reaches out and strokes the cream-coloured plastic. She turns and smiles at me. 'You always did manage to find such lovely things.'

We sit down, the three of us, at the kitchen table. I'm holding the mug of hot tea between my two hands. Over their heads I can see the window with its strip of fading light. Bare London trees on sky, the wall of the house next door, bricks dark with rain. A sparrow. A leaf. I rub my eyes. What time is it? A little shiver runs from my throat to my knees, all the way down. I have to get ready. I drink up the last dregs and push back my chair. I walk out of the room, leaving my mum and gran in a huddle over by the sink. They're picking things up and putting them down again, making little quiet exclaiming noises. As I walk out of the room I can still hear them admiring my gadgets – the cappuccino machine, the granite worktops, the new microwave – running their hands over each surface and asking each other questions in low excited voices. They don't even seem to see me leave.

But when I step out of the shower they're both there watching me, their two faces close together, slightly blurred through the steam. My gran looks quickly away. My mum says, 'You've got thinner, darling. Are you sure you've been...?' She bites back the rest of the sentence. I grab a towel and wrap it round me quickly, knotting the corners so it won't fall down. I lift up my hair and wind another, smaller towel round my head, twisting it into a turban. I push past them into the bedroom. I rub myself dry and find my clothes – underwear, tights, skirt, earrings. Then I feel in the plastic carrier bag and pull out the new top in its white tissue paper.

My mum's mouth falls open. She leans forward and touches a corner of the fabric, feeling it gently between thumb and forefinger. My gran leans over and slaps her smartly on the wrist and Mum draws back her hand. She turns to me and says the words almost in a whisper. 'This is in his honour, is it? You bought this because of him?'

My gran says, 'In our day we couldn't just go out and buy ourselves all kinds of finery whenever we felt like it.' She looks down her thin nose and says, 'In our day buttons were mother-of-pearl, or real bone.'

I turn on the TV and lie full-length on the sofa with the remote, changing from channel to channel. It's meaningless. On the screen a hand arranges something green on a plate, melts a knob of butter in a shiny pan. Anything to stop myself standing at the corner of the big bay window and watching for him to walk towards me up the dark street.

But Mum and Gran have no such scruples. My gran positions herself right in the bay, her eyes creased up with the effort of surveillance. My mum forgets herself entirely, kneeling in an armchair, her arms along its back and her chin resting on top of them like a little girl's.

'Here he is!' My mum can hardly keep the excitement out of her voice. My own stomach's gone all fluttery. I snap the TV off and go and join them at the window.

'Hello? Lizzie?' His voice in the entry-phone sounds tired. I try to remember how I thought he sounded.

'Hang on,' I say quickly. 'I'm all ready. I'll come down to you.' How can I do anything else, with the two of them buzzing round me like a couple of insects? I shrug on my coat, check the mirror briefly – hair, mascara, lipstick. I pick up my bag and sling it over my shoulder, almost hitting my gran on the cheek. I don't shout at her, I don't ask her why she keeps standing so close to me. I don't raise my voice to either of them. I look them both in the eye – Gran, Mum – and smile. I flick the light off. Outside the window the sky has gone from blue-grey to the orange haze of streetlamps, the straggly trees lit up from inside. Before they can stop me I'm in the hall.

But Gran's as quick on her feet as I am. She taps the box of the entry-phone twice with her fingernail. She puts her ear to it and listens. 'What is this, a telephone? Or some kind of wireless?'

My mum's looking at me, her eyes glinting in the red darkness. 'Was that him you were talking to just now? It was, wasn't it? You won't do anything silly, will you? Are you sure it's really him?'

We take the tube and walk to somewhere he knows, not far from West Kensington, a pub with some kind of snazzy glass extension where you can sit and pretend you're eating al fresco, a menu of overpriced ciabatta and sun-dried tomatoes and olive oil. We sit down at a round marble table surrounded by plants. The menu folder's shaking in my fingers. I put it down and hide my hands in my lap.

He sees me do it. He says, 'Is something the matter?'

I shake my head. 'It's nothing. It's just... '

He reaches for my hand and picks it up, stroking my fingers gently. 'This isn't supposed to be some obscure form of torture. If you don't want to be here with me, you don't have to stay.'

I try to laugh. 'Right.'

'What's the matter?'

'Nothing,' I say again.

He looks at me and smiles. He's puzzled. 'Have you decided?' He points to something on the menu. 'Shall we try the asparagus or do you fancy—'

It's out before I can stop myself: 'I think I'm just scared I... '

He waits for me to finish, but I can't. 'We're all scared,' he says. He leans back in his chair and calls the waiter over.

'Asparagus is fine,' I say quickly. 'And the risotto.' I wait until we're alone again. 'I just meant…' But I can't go on. 'I'm sorry. I think I just really need a drink.'

He doesn't say anything for a while. When the wine comes he tastes it and signals for the waiter to pour me a full glass. He's watching me closely. After a while he sits back in his chair and smiles. 'You mustn't expect too much of yourself. It takes a while. Even now I see an old geezer coming round the corner and sometimes for a split second I forget and think it's my dad. It's a bit like hunt-the-thimble. As soon as you stop looking it's right in front of your nose. On top of the clock usually.'

I turn round to follow the direction of his eyes, but there are only other people like us, their heads bent over their plates of food. 'My gran used to have a thimble.'

'Yeah, so did mine. I bet she kept it in her workbasket with one of those wooden mushroom things they used to darn socks with.'

'How did you…?' I meet his eyes and we both start to laugh.

*

'I do like that thing you're wearing.' He comes out with it quite naturally. Is he being ironic? But he's looking at me with real appreciation.

'Thank you.' My eyes prick suddenly and I start to fiddle with a corner of my crumpled napkin. 'You don't think the buttons let it down?'

'Buttons?' He hasn't even noticed there *are* any buttons.

'I did just wonder if they were a bit too contemporary, a bit brash – if I should think about changing them.'

'What would you change them for?'

He's got me there. 'Bone?'

'Does anyone still make things out of bone?' He takes the card and receipt the waiter's holding out to him and slips them into his wallet with a nod.

'Or mother-of-pearl?' I say. But he's not listening. I stand up and allow him to dress me in my coat, lifting my hair out over the collar. Then we're making our way out between the tables, back into the dark street. He puts his arm round my shoulders. Under a streetlight he pulls me round and looks at me closely. He picks up a strand of my hair and fans it out with his other hand.

I make a face. 'It's just the light,' I tell him. 'It isn't really that red. My mum had red hair when she was young.'

He hugs me suddenly and it's hard to let him go. When we reach my building his arm's still round my shoulder.

The door swings open on darkness. The bulb must have blown. *Black as Newgate's knocker*, Gran would have said. I turn and face him but it's hard to read his expression. 'Do you want to come up?'

'Do you want me to come up?'

'What do you think?'

He pulls me gently towards him.

He follows me up the stairs in silence. I open the lounge door and go in. The remote's still face-downwards on the floor next to the sofa. There's an empty glass on the mantelpiece where I left it, half visible in the glow from outside.

I hang up his leather jacket in the hall, next to my coat. Then I go into the kitchen and switch on the spots. 'Something else to drink?' I ask him.

'What have you got?'

'Wine. Whisky. V8 juice. Milk.'

Behind me my gran's voice says, '*V8 juice?* What's that when it's at home?' She sounds scornful. She's sitting over in the corner, next to the microwave, with my mum at her elbow.

'You always used to like milk,' my mum says to me. 'I used to give you warm milk sometimes when you were little. It was supposed to be comforting. We needed it, just after the War. They told us it was good for our teeth. Why don't you give him milk?'

He seems to consider. He stands there in the doorway with his hands in his pockets. 'Actually, I don't think I really need anything. But thanks.'

'He's well behaved, anyway,' my gran says.

My mum's looking anxious.

'See how polite he is?' My gran's watching him intently. 'And considerate. Consideration's not to be sneezed at, in a man.'

He reaches out and takes my hand and pulls me gently towards the bedroom. We could be sleepwalking. Somehow, before I know it, I'm under the duvet and he's standing in front of me in only his socks and underpants. My mum and my gran have taken the two Ikea chairs and lined them up by the bed, in the best possible position. They're not going to miss a single moment. They lean forward expectantly, my mum almost holding her breath.

'He's a fine figure of a man,' my gran says. 'He's got the necessary.'

My mum's twisting nervously on her seat. She raises one hand to her mouth to chew at a hangnail or a bit of loose skin. 'Darling... ' she says to me. 'You are going to be careful?'

He's taking his socks off one by one, standing first on one leg and then the other, then stooping to pull down his underpants.

'We used to call it "standing to attention".' My gran's voice has an odd sort of croak in it.

'Did you really? In the sixties some of us still used to call this whole thing "making love".' My mum doesn't know whether to laugh or try and be serious for my sake.

And then he's beside me under the quilt and they can't see us. I can feel his skin on mine, the warm smooth expanse of him, the weird familiarity and strangeness of it. The way he smells – of himself and only himself – a smell that's nothing like anything or anyone I remember.

And he's inside me in that darkness, together we're sliding and shivering, peeling the dark like an onion, layer on layer. We're in a place where 'alone' has no meaning, where all the people who've ever died are breathing inside us, skin on skin. *Hold them back*, I'm saying to myself. *Hold them back*. And somehow I do. So that in the end when they come they're quiet and almost apologetic, they've been dead so long. I'm shivering, there are so many of them. My mouth's full of them – their skin and saliva and hair and semen, silk and sea and ash. Mother-of-pearl. Bones.

When it's over I'm crying. Slowly the room slips back into focus: the light shapes of the chairs, flowers on the sill, and beyond the glass that red cold glow, the world. A dog barking. Drunken voices, a woman singing. His face turned away from mine. Asleep. What now? I reach out and touch his shoulder.

'Ssst!' my gran says. She's standing at the end of the bed, my mum a slightly taller shadow at her side. My gran says, 'We didn't do any of that if we weren't married. We didn't even know it existed.'

I raise my eyebrows. She says, 'I didn't know about any of that until my wedding night. That was the first time I ever saw a man's rod and tackle. It was quite a shock, I can tell you.'

My mum doesn't say anything much. I try to meet her eyes, but she's looking studiously away.

My gran says, 'They didn't tell us about any of it. When we asked where babies came from they said God came and left them like gifts on your pillow.' I look at her. *Who is this woman?* She's far too old to be my gran. I don't even remember my real gran that well, I was only little, but I know this sour old woman's nothing like her at all.

And then my mum looks at me. She's younger than she was when she died, and rosy, as if she's only just got out of bed herself. A little wisp of reddish hair floats across her cheek and she brushes it back. 'Darling.' She says it so softly I'm not sure I've even heard. 'Are you quite sure you're going to be all right?'

Sharks

The metal's cold under her fingers. She turns the butterfly handle and pulls the box open, then slides the visitors' book out of its holder and begins to leaf through it, puzzling at the foreign handwriting. Sometimes there's something printed clearly, in capitals. A name that isn't as strange as the others – somewhere she's actually been to. Once, the name of her own home town. And the thankyous. An almost endless procession of thankyous in three different languages, stretching back into the past, the remaining blank pages already waiting to receive them. And the rain running down over her hands, wetting the paper. You can see from the blurred blue lines of some of the writing that this isn't the first time the book's been rained on. There must have been other days, all kinds of days, days when you'd be able to open the book and the names would be almost invisible in the bright sun.

She walks slowly back the way she came, between waterlogged fields and pollarded willows, past a sudden sloping hopfield that reminds her of home. She turns round and stands looking downhill, back at the gently undulating landscape of fields and packed red roofs and pointed spires.

Because home is exactly what she's come here to get away from. She only has to close her eyes and it's all still there waiting − the classroom with its long windows, the grouped tables, the kids leaning across one another to talk, or jumping up with any half-baked excuse. And their work − each badly spelt word and clumsy illustration a major achievement − pinned up everywhere, all over the walls. Even here, the voices still reach her − *But last week you... This fucking... What does she think she's...* And she's had enough. A week here in France, to get herself together. And when she goes back she'll give in her notice, leave them all to get on with it. She'll start to remember what it feels like not to be perpetually harassed and shouted at. Be someone else. Do something more useful with her life.

When she touches the tiled wall at the deep end she looks up and sees a pair of knees. Above them, a small face, a little kid of ten or eleven, leaning forward, watching her intently. 'How do you manage?' he says.

At first she doesn't understand what he's asking. She hangs on the side of the pool, getting her breath. Then the French words begin to sink in. 'What?' she says. 'Manage what?'

'Goggles.' He's pointing to his own face, freckled and grinning, the band of black rubber pushed up into his hair. 'How do you get them to stop steaming up? I can't see anything with mine. Is it something you do?' He leans down over the side, waving the goggles in her face so she can see the condensation. Suddenly she gets the message. She finds herself smiling back. 'Don't you know the trick?'

'What trick?'

'You spit on them. Then you rub your finger over the lenses – like this.' She takes her own off and shows him. 'Then you sort of swirl them round in the water.'

'And then what?'

'Then you put them on.'

He's looking at her doubtfully. All the same, he takes his goggles off his head and spits into them half-heartedly, giving them a perfunctory rub.

Every time she walks she seems to pass them – small manicured squares of grass, the lines of white gravestones evenly spaced. Only here and there, where the ground has shifted slightly, one that leans almost imperceptibly towards its neighbour, a few inches to the right or left.

And each time she passes she goes in. She sits and looks at the stones until they're not stones but clean folded sheets, or bread, or the white tiles of an upside-down roof.

And each night in her dreams the young faces come to her, tangled up with the hooting of owls.

It's starting to get to her. She's feeling slightly sick, somewhere in the pit of her stomach, deep down. She doesn't even know if she'll be able to swim. The ladder's slippery under her hands.

She lowers herself carefully rung by rung. As she reaches the bottom the water rocks suddenly, as if something's exploded deep under the surface, a commotion of bubbles rising and breaking. Next to her, a small face bobs up, spitting out water like a gargoyle, grinning in her direction. It's shouting something. Against the noise of the pool she can't hear it. Then she makes out the words. 'It worked!'

She's swallowed a mouthful of water. She kicks out, spluttering. 'What?'

'Your trick!'

And she recognises the little boy, his hair plastered to his head and darkened by the water. 'Really?'

'Yup. I spat in them, like you said. See? And they don't mist up any more. It's brilliant! I can go right down to the bottom and see all the feet and everything, and people's hair, it's like seaweed, and the lines of the tiles.'

'Great!' she says. 'If there's a shark, you can tip me off.'

For a few strokes he swims along beside her, trying to keep up. 'Wait for me!' he's saying. 'Let me come with you!'

It's ludicrous. She's come here for exercise – her 44 lengths – the 44 lengths that'll keep her physically and mentally in shape. And he's barely even treading water, he's struggling somewhere behind her, just about level with her feet. And she's already striking out towards the shallow end, where older kids are throwing a rubber ring and trying to balance on the submerged ropes.

But something makes her stop and turn round. And there he is, like a puppy, paddling frantically with his arms, puffing and blowing. 'You know...' He gasps it out between breaths. 'There aren't actually any sharks.'

She almost chokes again as she turns and waits for him to catch up.

On her last day she decides to walk somewhere flatter. She's spent the whole week exploring the hills and it's the hills that remind her of home. She starts out from the little town in a mist of fine rain.

She pulls her hood up and keeps walking, the rain driving into the oval space where her face is, finding her neck. By the time she reaches the graveyard on the outskirts she's already so cold her stiff fingers can hardly get a grip on the box's metal handle.

She flicks through the pages quickly. Read one and you've read them all, that's the way she tends to find herself thinking these days. *Thank you, thank you.* She's worn down with all this gratitude. What can you do with it, when the dazed, uncomprehending 17- and 18-year-olds it's meant for are all so very dead?

But then, something different, a whole series of short entries, in adolescent handwriting. She forces herself to concentrate. Kettering, the addresses say. Where the hell is Kettering? She tries to visualise a map of Britain. She turns back to the laconic messages, and starts to smile. 'Moving,' someone's written – a young boy, probably. In English they must be doing Owen and Sassoon, the *Up the Line to Death* anthology. The 'moving' is echoed in other places further down the page. Someone, a girl, has written 'macabre'. Someone else has written 'shocking'. She looks for other words but doesn't find them. After all, the words these kids have used are not so far from the vocabulary of the kids she teaches in her own classes.

And then one that makes her laugh aloud. 'School trip.' Just that. No personal reaction, no explanation, nothing. It has to have been written by a boy. And it's perfect, it says everything. Even without trying, she can see the sixteen-year-old kid who wrote it, his lowered face, his blue eyes looking out at her mutinously from under overhanging hair. He could be one of her own.

The grass is very green. Already among the graves there are one or two flowers – purple polyanthus, such a dark colour she hadn't even noticed. It's still raining, harder than ever, but there's a patch of yellow in the hedge over by the road, a few fat buds among the leaves of what must be daffodils. Another time or season and it would look quite different. She wonders what it would look like through the eyes of the kids in her class.

Pain

The day before Sarah was due to go skiing with Matt, one of her back molars started to play up. It was only a twinge if she bit down on something suddenly, or an ache when she drank something hot, it didn't bother her that much. And it was as much as she could do now to tie up the loose ends at work and think about buying her sunscreen and tube-socks. She'd get it seen to as soon as she got back.

And Matt would look after her. He was such a sweetie. It was three years now since they'd started seeing each other and they hardly ever fell out about anything. And he was attractive too – with freckles and a big open grin, and greenish grey eyes. It amazed her that her friends were less than enthusiastic. 'What do you see in him?' Her friends would look at her in concern, their eyebrows coming together in a frown.

They'd been an item for three years. When they went out they always went out together. Friends who invited her were in the habit of asking Matt too. For nearly three years now they'd been taking all their holidays together because that seemed the most natural thing.

Yet somehow lately she'd found herself thinking of other possibilities, other lives – unmanned cars and boats, holidays in remote cottages on the edge of the Yorkshire Moors or the west coast of Wales. 'What do you mean, it isn't going anywhere?' Her friends waited for her to say something more definite. But she couldn't put her finger on what it was. Somehow she always remembered the good times. And when she tried to imagine breaking up with him she could always see his face.

'Why don't you do something you haven't done together yet?' her friend Louise said. 'How about rock-climbing? Or skiing? You might get to see him in a totally different light.'

She loved the mountains. She loved snow. She loved Austria. She loved Matt, even if it wasn't going to last for ever, even if they might split up eventually. Maybe by the end of the fortnight she'd just about know her own feelings and finishing it would be easier. She could even savour these last few days with him, knowing they probably were the last. She'd have memories, and photographs of white peaks and cable-cars and kids with panda eyes to show to her friends when she got back. She arranged the hired ski-suit in her suitcase with the new socks and gloves and woolly hat and sunglasses, pushing a packet of Nurofen deep into the crack next to the paperback she'd bought for the homeward flight.

Most of the other chalet guests were families, and seemed to know one another already. At tea-time they'd help themselves to scones with jam and cream, or enormous slabs of cake. The kids would take over the small seating-area in front of the log fire, messing about with their Gameboys, flopping all over one another, discussing their favourite bands. Or they'd rummage among the packs of cards and dominoes, the old-fashioned board-games the chalet provided, their sunburnt faces clustered together in complicated deals as they bought or sold Piccadilly, the Old Kent Road, utilities. Someone would put a hotel on Mayfair and the rest would groan, raising their eyes to the exposed beams. She and Matt would retire to their room and sit with their feet up on the rail of the balcony, drinking whisky out of tooth-glasses. Afterwards they'd make love on one of the narrow beds.

There was only one other couple they might have something in common with. The woman was small and slight and rather shy, the man more outgoing. They were called Kirsty and Alistair. Experienced skiers, apparently, both of them. The first evening they found themselves at the same table, exchanging skiing anecdotes and thumbnail sketches of their lives at home. After dinner they decided to check out the Wild Boar. In the noise of people shouting over the jukebox and the smell of mulled wine and woodsmoke it felt as if they'd all known one another for years. Alistair turned to Sarah. 'Have you put your names down for the tour?'

'I'm sorry?'

'Tomorrow morning. With the reps. It's not a lesson. They're not allowed to teach. You just follow them. But they know the snow and they know the mountain. They can show you where the best runs are.'

'Great.' She looked at Matt. 'Doesn't that sound amazing?'

'Our first morning? Do you really think we're up to it?'

'Oh, come on.'

'It's okay. They won't make you do anything you can't handle.' Alistair's big face glowed. 'They take you to the top and give you a choice of at least two ways down. You can take the red, or even the blue if you're feeling... if you're only just getting your ski-legs.' He spread his hands flat on the table, grinning at them both.

Kirsty was smiling too, in her quiet way. 'It's nothing to be nervous of. Really. You wouldn't catch me doing anything dangerous. Come with us. You'll get to know the resort. You won't regret it, I promise.'

118

Sarah looked at Matt again. 'Well? What do you think?' she said.

The next morning they were all up early, everyone scrabbling for breakfast in a chaos of kids in T-shirts and dangling salopette-straps. Kirsty and Alistair were just visible on the far side of the dining-room. Matt and Sarah ate their boiled eggs, drank down their coffee and pushed back their chairs. 'Well, you let us in for this,' Matt said.

They followed the others up on the T-bar, Sarah struggling to keep her skis straight in the twin channels, unbalanced by Matt's greater height and weight, the bar threatening to throw her every time the cable went slack. They passed through the shadow of the pine-woods where the skis hissed across ice and the pylons were bearded with tiny icicles, up to the top where there was an open view over unbroken sky and snow. The wind cut across them, flicking up horse-tails of white powder along the ridges, making the air all round them glitter. She could feel the cold on her teeth, on one tooth in particular, clean and clear as a whistle. God! She clamped her mouth shut as she bent down to tighten the clasps of her boots and the ache receded. And then they were off: the rep in front and Kirsty – surprisingly – just on his heels, easy and graceful in her slate-blue suit, Alistair solid and heavier in black. The three of them went lightly over the top and out of sight. She and Matt followed, neither of them really ahead of the other, meeting and crossing at each traverse with a shout of dismay, but somehow making it, somehow getting to the bottom, stopping hard in a rush of snow, half-staggering into each other's arms. 'Told you!' she said. Matt's face was pink from the stinging air. He lifted his sunglasses and wiped the tears from the corners of his eyes.

After that the four of them were free to go together, without the rep. They knew it now. They knew which lifts fed which runs, where you could cut across to a different network, where the snow would be melting in the sun and where it was likely to be icy, the places where yesterday's melt had turned to glass, half-hidden in the mountain's shadow.

Kirsty swooped ahead like a blue bird, the rest of them racing to keep up, sweating under their jackets, their legs shaking whenever they stood still. It wasn't as clear as yesterday. The sky was full of small white clouds like crazy paving that seemed to have moved slightly closer every time they stopped and looked up. 'My God!' Sarah heard herself say.

Matt mimicked her. 'My God! Just look at those little bitty clouds!'

She pretended to punch him in the face and he lay down in the snow and rolled over, laughing, like an ungainly insect. She fell on top of him and pummelled him in the chest, knocking off his glasses. Their skis tangled and one of hers came off, slithering fifteen feet lower and stopping on its side. He trudged to get it and brought it back to her. He positioned it where she could step into it. He pulled her up and knocked the caked snow from the bottom of her boot with his stick.

They took the next slope even faster, to catch up. The snow rushed to meet them, and then the highest scrubby fringes of the first trees. The pain sang suddenly in Sarah's head again. She must have been skiing with her mouth open. Sheer delight must have been making her smile.

By the time they caught the others up the little blue cracks between the clouds had closed up entirely. There were no shadows. The humps and hollows under their skis had become invisible, the mountain opposite blotted out by cloud. And the horizon itself was slowly disappearing as they watched, the white of the snow bleeding into the white of the sky. A few snowflakes fell round them quietly. She turned to Alistair. 'Which way now?'

He waved his pole in the direction of the valley. 'This top bit's red and blue. They fork about halfway down. The red's fairly direct. And the blue goes off to the side, behind that...' They looked where he pointed, but whatever it was had gone. 'Whichever. We can take either. I'll go first. I'll wait just at the fork, and when we get there we can decide.'

He went ahead. Kirsty hung back with them this time, not so confident in these conditions, stopping at the edge of the run with each traverse. Now all they could see was one another. They stayed close, almost on one another's ski-tips. There was no sign of Alistair.

And then suddenly the ground under their feet was steeper. Suddenly the traverses were shorter, the run narrower, the unseen trees closing in on either side. Before Sarah had had a chance to turn, a tree-trunk loomed right at her out of the mist. She stopped dead and fell over in the piled snow at the edge. She struggled up again quickly. She had to keep going. She mustn't lose sight of the others.

Matt was just ahead. Through the fog of falling snow she could see his grin. 'It's all right. It can't be far,' he said. 'We must somehow've got on to the black. But it'll be all right. At least it'll take us straight down.'

'True,' Sarah said. Her teeth were chattering. There was ice on the side where the trees had cast their long shadows. You could hear it grating on the bottoms of the skis as you turned. And there were moguls. You couldn't see them, but you could feel them: one minute you were up, your feet almost leaving the ground, and the next you were thrown backwards. Like feeling the skin of the earth wrinkle suddenly in the dark. The white dark. She compressed her lips firmly, not letting the cold in.

It was Matt she came on first. He was standing over something, a blue body spreadeagled over an extra-large bump, the head tipped backwards: Kirsty. As Sarah reached them, the body lifted its head and smiled. 'Are you okay?' Sarah said.

'I think so. Only I've lost a ski.'

'Where is it?' Around them the white closed in. 'Wait. I'll go down for it,' Matt said.

He pushed off into the mist. A moment later his voice came back. 'I've got it.'

'I'll come down,' Kirsty said. She stood up carefully and began to edge sideways down the slope. But at the first step she cried out and crumpled suddenly. She bumped and slid downhill, her gloved fingers clutching at the icy faces of the moguls and scraping away.

Sarah was alone. She side-slipped towards them inch by inch and slowly their two shapes came to meet her out of the fog, Matt standing with the ski in his hand, Kirsty on the ground at his feet. 'It's no good,' Kirsty was saying. 'It's my shoulder. Something must be broken. It hurts too much.'

For a while they just stood there looking down at her, side by side, snow falling all round them. Matt had a snowflake in his left eyebrow. They dug their poles into the white crust to stop their feet sliding out from under them.

'Don't worry, Kirsty,' Matt said. He was leaning over her, stroking the top of her head gently through the hat with his gloved hand. 'I remember this place from yesterday. The chairlift runs right over us, just above our heads almost. You can't see it in this, but it's not more than a few yards away. If we shout, someone's got to hear us.'

Kirsty didn't say anything. She'd closed her eyes. Sarah strained her ears to hear any noise in the sky, anyone or anything that might be there. She thought perhaps she could make out a distant, muffled whirr. 'Go on, then,' she said. 'Shout.'

Matt shouted. For an hour he shouted, at regular intervals. For two hours. And finally, just as the fog was beginning to lift slightly, there was a cry in answer. The low cloud thinned and opened, and the grey spire of a pylon came out of it, cables, a chair just passing overhead, people's legs dangling. 'Hello!' Matt shouted. And the answer came back, faintly, in a language she didn't understand. She dropped her poles and began to wave her arms in circles. 'Help!' she called. 'One of us is hurt! Help! *Help!*'

Twenty minutes later the mountain-rescue people were there, two strong Austrians with the blood-wagon zigzagging between them. The clouds had lifted completely now and the men approached almost directly, almost straight down the mountain, stopping beside them with a rasp. They wrapped Kirsty in something that looked like tinfoil and lifted her gently on to the sledge. They immobilised her limbs with straps from head to toe. Then they headed off into the valley, making it look so easy. They guided the red thing that was Kirsty almost straight down.

Matt and Sarah followed more slowly. It was almost easy, now they could see the contours. Easy when you could see where you were, the bumps to turn on, the fringe of dark trees. The sheer mogul-run levelled out almost immediately, opening into a wide bowl of fresh snow.

They were halfway through dinner when Alistair came over. 'She's fine,' he said. 'She's resting. She didn't feel like eating anything. But she's okay. She broke her arm, high up, near the shoulder. Too high for plaster – they've strapped it up. They've given us some pain-killers, just for tonight. We're flying back to London tomorrow. We thought we might as well.'

'I'm sorry,' Sarah said.

'I know.' Alistair turned to Matt. 'I can't understand how we got on that black run instead of the blue. But these things happen. Thank you for what you did.'

'We didn't do anything.' She reached under the table for Matt's hand and squeezed it. 'We did what anyone would have done. I'm sorry you're both leaving.' She looked at Alistair and smiled. 'I hope the pain-killers do the trick.'

The rest of the week, the two of them were on their own. The sky was clear now and it was hard to remember the grey landscape that had greeted them on their arrival. At night the high peaks gleamed in the moonlight. The bottle of whisky was finished and they couldn't seem to muster the energy to go to a shop and buy more.

Once they played a game of Monopoly with the teenagers grouped round the fireplace. Sarah had all the stations, but somehow she ended up losing anyway, selling every last house, turning her cards face downwards one by one. In the grate the flames streamed. A log collapsed in a jet of sparks. Matt was winning, rubbing his hands together, buying property, building hotels, getting himself out of gaol whenever he felt like it. They'd play on for hours yet. She stood up and stretched and yawned. Then she went upstairs. When Matt opened the door and turned on the bathroom light she rolled over and felt herself drift back into sleep.

*

On their last evening they decided to do something different. So far they'd hardly even tasted the night-life. It was something to do with meeting Alistair and Kirsty and then the accident and having to say goodbye. Somehow since that first night none of the pubs in the village had looked inviting. 'Let's take the road and see what it's like a bit further down,' Matt said.

'How can we?'

'We could just walk down along the road. I think I noticed a disco-bar on the way in. It was about two miles.'

'Are you sure? Can we be bothered to walk that far?'

'It isn't a big deal. If we don't manage to reach it, we can always just come back. As long as we're together.'

They walked down the road in single file, listening for the sound of an engine, watching for headlights. The clumps of snow at the roadside had melted and refrozen. Most of the time they walked on the road itself because it was easier. Halfway down, there was a short tunnel that ended in a series of arches hung with icicles, gaping suddenly open on snow.

The bar was at the top end of a reservoir, overlooking the water with its white crust. Inside it was almost empty. Tonight there was no sign of any disco, though there was a pile of black boxes and cables in one corner. Just a couple of men in jackets and turtlenecks, smoking. She chose a table on the inside, away from the window, where it would be warmer. She ordered mulled wine, then schnapps. Matt was drinking beer. She thought she could already see something rueful in the way he looked at her, something almost nostalgic. Perhaps this wasn't going to be all that difficult. Her jaw gave a twinge suddenly and she put a hand to her cheek.

'Are you okay?' His face in the dim light was full of concern. He put his hand over hers. She could just make out the freckles under his eyes.

She swallowed. She'd rehearsed this so often. Whatever she tried always sounded hopelessly melodramatic. 'Matt, I'm really sorry,' she said.

He didn't move. His fingers didn't clench on the sides of the glass. He was looking down at the table-top, its oilskin cloth streaked with beer where he'd slopped it, scarred in one place by a cigarette-burn. He looked up at her suddenly.

'I'm really sorry, Matt. It's been three years. I think I'm just... ready to move on.'

'Is there someone else?' The tone of his voice made her sit up. He still had a sense of parody, anyway. It couldn't be too bad if he could do that all right. What should she tell him? Was it better to answer yes or no? She said, 'Not really.'

*

He downed his drink quickly. He shrugged on his coat and waited while she put on her own. At the door he lifted his gloved hands and brought them back to his sides. 'I don't get it,' he said.

She looked past him at the heaped dirty snow at the roadside. Her eyes filled with tears. 'I don't know. We just... We don't... We aren't going anywhere.'

'Where do you want to go?'

'I don't know,' she said again.

'Is it about kids? Are you thinking you might want to have kids?'

She shook her head. 'I'm not sure. Yes. Possibly.'

'We could have children.'

'No, I...' She pulled the collar of her jacket up over her chin so the cold wouldn't get to her tooth. 'Let's talk about it when we get back to England, okay? You'll have got used to the idea by then.'

They walked back almost in silence. They groped their way through the tunnel, their boots echoing on the surface of the road, the walls above them glittering. 'Look,' Matt said. Beside them a dark archway opened on almost the whole length of the far ridge. The mountains gleamed, white in the moonlight, separated by sharp shadows. Matt's face in the pale glow was puzzled, sceptical almost. He reached into her pocket for her hand and held it. After a few seconds she took it away.

*

As soon as she got home, she made an appointment with her dentist. 'You have to take care of yourself,' her friends told her, and she believed them. 'Just because you've broken up with Matt, it doesn't mean you can let yourself go.' The dentist probed her open mouth and a note of pain went through her, thin and high and white, leaving her shaking. He grunted, muttered something to his assistant. He adjusted the lamp slightly so it no longer shone right into her eyes. 'I'm going to have to fill this. I'm sorry.'

She uncrossed her ankles. 'I know.'

'Would you like an injection?'

'Will I need an injection?'

'It's six of one and half a dozen of the other. You might.'

'Okay, then. I will.' She waited as he prepared the anaesthetic. Very consciously she relaxed her hands on the armrests, looking at the framed print on the far wall. A picture of a path winding towards purple mountains, tasteless and sentimental. When the needle came she hardly even felt it go in. Already her upper lip was beginning to go numb, a sensation like cold spreading under her nose. It wasn't anything to get steamed up about, after all. Dentists did this kind of thing to people every day.

And then suddenly everything was falling away. Her heart was pounding in her chest. She could feel the colour draining from her face. How stupid! How very stupid! She wasn't going to let herself do this! She wasn't going to faint, she wasn't going to move a muscle. She forced herself to fix her eyes on something straight ahead. In the picture the mountains came nearer, closing in on her, crushing her bone by bone.

But before she knew it her dentist was leaning over her. The chair had flattened out, tipped backwards, her head towards the ground. His hand was on her arm. 'Bad decision,' he said.

In a moment she felt better. Her heart was quieter. The white walls of the room were ordinary again. He was looking down at her, and her mind was her own. 'How did you know?' she asked him.

'We're trained to watch for it. Sometimes the anaesthetic hits a vein. It happens very rarely.'

She spat into the basin and watched the few drops of blood spiral down into the hole. She felt okay really. The tooth was all done. Nothing had happened, nothing particularly unpleasant, anyway. She just couldn't quite believe how quickly her dentist had reacted, how he'd seen right through her, how he'd known at once when the mountains in the picture had come forward out of the frame.

My Father's Shoes

The day of the interview was also the day I buried my father's shoes. I drove over to Mum's early. She started sniffing and clinging to me as soon as I came in the door. 'You've got to stop this,' I told her. 'He isn't ever going to come back. You've got to start pulling yourself together. You're not that old. If you only made some sort of effort, you could still have a good life.'

She took a step backwards. She pulled out a tissue and blew her nose. Then she turned away from me and started filling a saucepan under the cold tap. There was no way I could make myself heard over the drumming of the water. If that's how she wanted it, fine. That was her problem. I went upstairs to the big front bedroom they'd shared.

She still slept in the double bed. She hadn't got round to pulling up the covers and I could see where she'd been lying, on her own side, next to the space where the sheets were still unwrinkled. On his bedside table the clock alarm glowed red. For all I knew his pyjamas were still under the pillow, neatly folded. And along the wall next to the wardrobe was the row of shoes.

There were even more of them than I remembered. They stood in neat pairs, the heels towards me, the toes turned to the wall. Office shoes, walking shoes, the old rubber galoshes he hadn't worn since I was a small boy. The beige canvas shoes he wore when he and Mum were in Spain together. I slipped my own shoes off and tried them on. He and I were almost the same size. I stooped to pick up the worn-out brogues he called his gardening shoes, though I'd never actually seen him wearing them. In all likelihood he'd inherited them from his own father. They used to be a family joke, when he was alive.

I gathered them all up to put them in a black plastic rubbish-bag. As I took hold of them my fingers entered the place where his feet had been and I could feel the shape of his bones under my hands. Our feet weren't that different – his just a bit broader and nobbier, that's all. The black plastic mouth hung slack. His shoes were heavy. The bag sagged, threatening to burst. I twisted it at the neck and carried it downstairs.

She was still in the kitchen, her head bent over the sink, her back shaking rhythmically as she scraped at something with a little knife. I let myself out the front way and went down to the bottom of the garden, beyond the apple-trees, where she couldn't see what I was doing. I got the big spade out of the shed and cut away a neat rectangle of turf. I dug the hole as deep as I could manage. Then I tipped the shoes into it and shook the bag over them. Something fell out – an insole, the tag from one of the laces – and I gave the bag one last shake to make quite sure. I used the spade to push the earth back in over them. When I replaced the turf you could hardly see anything. Just a neat incision, a slight unevenness. I banged at the bag to get all the air out and slipped it into my pocket. She wouldn't even know.

Over lunch she was better. She was trying, obviously. She'd taken my little speech to heart. She'd roasted a chicken, cooked new potatoes and cauliflower, the way she used to every Sunday when I was small. The gravy was thick and brown, just as he liked it. 'So what time's your interview?' she said.

'Four-fifteen.'

'You're not going like that, are you?'

'Mum,' I said. 'You're living in the past. People don't dress up to go to University these days. When did you last see a student in a suit?'

She looked at me dubiously but she didn't say anything. I helped her wash up. It was almost three. In a minute I'd have to be thinking about going. I went upstairs to the bathroom to shave. I should make that much effort for them at least.

I used my dad's old electric razor. I stretched the skin of my cheek and ran the blunt old thing up and down. Over the hum of the motor I could hear her in the toilet on the other side of the wall. Then she came out. She must have gone into the bedroom for something. I heard her shriek.

'What have you done with them?'

I came out on to the landing, the razor still buzzing in my hand. 'What?'

'His shoes. Where are they? What have you done with his shoes?'

'I've taken them away,' I told her. 'It's not good for you to live like that, still surrounded by his things.'

'Where did you put them?' She was actually shaking. She came up and clung to me. She clung to me. Her knees were so wobbly I was actually having to hold her up. The label of her blouse stuck up at the back.

I pushed her away gently. 'We had to do something about them sometime. You weren't going to leave them there for ever.'

She didn't say anything. The tears squeezed out from under her closed eyelids.

'It wasn't healthy. What do you think it does to me, every time I come over, to see them all lined up like that?'

She almost crumpled then. I held her in my arms and rocked her gently, her soft hair on my face, my neck wet with her tears. I could feel her sagging, her weight throwing me off-balance until I stumbled sideways and almost fell.

But I had to go. 'You *will* be all right, won't you?'

She nodded, reaching into the pocket of her baggy old trousers for a fresh tissue. She blew her nose with one hand, holding on to the banisters with the other. She was still looking down on me as I closed the front door.

'But what do you want to go to University for?' That's what he'd said to me, years ago, when I was eighteen. 'You can learn what you need to on the job. That's what I did. Why would you want to waste three years doing nothing? When you get out you'll only find you're three rungs below everyone else. All they do at those places is drink and mess about and go to parties. Do you really want to spend three years of your life just messing about?'

I put my foot down on the accelerator and drove. In ten minutes I was on the M20. Then I was driving up a steep hill, the town falling away behind me, woods and fields on either side. My heart was hammering suddenly. I hadn't had time to prepare myself. I hadn't read any of the right books. I wouldn't be able to answer any of the questions they might decide to put to me. I couldn't believe

I'd frittered away the morning on my mother's back lawn with a bag of old shoes and a garden spade. I reached the top and coasted down, past the showground, past the garage, past the Three Squirrels. Once I hit a rough place in the road and the car bounced suddenly. I took the filter for the M2, slowing almost to thirty as the slip-road bent sharply south, then east. They'd have to take me as they found me. I might not know anything, but I could cut a mean piece of turf.

I arrived just as the young woman in front of me was leaving. After a few minutes they called me in. There were a couple of them, a man and a woman, sitting there with a sheaf of papers on their knees. They asked me to sit down and pointed at a low chair. Outside the window a weeping willow was like a green tent full of sun. 'Mr Heaseman?' I nodded as they went through the introductions. 'What was it that attracted you to this programme?' The woman looked at me and smiled.

I started to tell them. I told them about the books I'd read in my childhood, and the other books I'd read since Dad died. If they disapproved of my choices they didn't show it. They questioned me about them anyway. They asked me about the stories and the characters and why they mattered. They asked me about how you entered a character's thoughts, how you knew when you were supposed to be in sympathy and when you were meant to keep your distance. And somehow we got on to books about fathers and sons.

And then it was easy. I told them everything – how I'd cut away the square of grass so neatly that when I put it back the join was hardly visible, how the shoes had gone into the hole in pairs, two of each kind, like animals into the ark, how the different styles had slid over one another in a great shapeless heap. And they sat there and smiled at me. I told myself they weren't laughing unkindly, but underneath I was pretty sure their smiles were smiles of scorn.

They waited for me to finish. Then the man said, 'Just to come back to *Ulysses* for a moment...' That was when I looked down at my feet and saw I was wearing my father's shoes.

They were the brown slip-ons he kept for the beach, with woven string insets in the top, an old man's shoes, faded and scuffed from whole summers spent scrambling over sliding stones. I had a sudden picture of him as he'd been then, the brim of the fishing-hat shading his eyes, his big warm hand almost enclosing mine, his trousers rolled up over his hairy calves. He was showing me something – a hermit crab waving its half-transparent whiskers in the crevice of a submerged rock. It was so delicate you could only just make it out, the little mauve-and-black-striped legs scrabbling frantically against a clump of rusty weed. I screwed up my eyes to see what he saw. But already the two lecturers were standing up and shaking my hand, signalling that the interview was over. I nodded. I walked quickly to the door and out into the corridor, then along it, towards the outside.

The branches of the weeping willow came right down to the ground. I crossed the square of grass and slipped in under them quickly. I lit a cigarette and watched the smoke drifting upwards through the leaves. I'd made a complete fool of myself, there was no doubt about it. I knew nothing about James Joyce, nothing about Updike, nothing about Greek mythology, nothing about father-and-son relationships in serious books. And I'd actually been sitting there talking to them in my Dad's old shoes. It was comical. I was starting to laugh.

It didn't matter. All round me the leaves of the willow were a pale green waterfall, rippling slightly in the breeze, full of light. I'd get there eventually. If not this time, then next. I slipped the shoes off and yanked at my socks. They were sticking to me with sweat. I rolled them up and stuffed them inside the battered string toes. Then I came out of the tree and walked barefoot towards my car across the grass.

For You

When Sister Manning ushers the carol-singers into the lounge, every single one of them is beaming. There are eleven of them: eight adults and three children. Eleven smiles on full beam, eleven pairs of feet marching in single file, a chorus of eleven greetings full of barely-suppressed joy.

The adults come first. A woman is leading them, her chest out, her cream satin blouse straining. Her black lace-ups seem to be marking a rhythm the others have to follow. Behind her, another, younger woman with red hair plaited on top of her head, fastened invisibly somewhere behind her pink ears. A man in a suit and tie carries a zither in one hand and a tambourine in the other. His finger-nails are black and splitting. His unremitting smile is a jumble of stained teeth. And the others come after, carrying song-books and leaflets.

And with them the children. Two small boys are holding lanterns mounted on long sticks. They walk stiffly, mesmerised by the lit candles inside, their smiles giving way to brief anxiety as the flames flicker and threaten to go out in the draught from the outer door. And the girl, slightly older, taller, plumper, with red cheeks and a cloak of curtain-netting fastened by a brooch in front, a wreath of tinsel pinned on top of her yellow hair.

They pass through in single file to the far end and stand grouped by the artificial Christmas-tree. They beam. The man with the teeth gives out the instruments. One of the others distributes the song-books. They turn to face the old people. They look round slowly, embracing the whole room. Sister Manning has retreated into the kitchen doorway. They nod at her, then at the room in general. 'Peace be with you, brother, sister,' they say. 'Peace be yours this Christmastide. The Christ is born. He is come down among us to save us all.' The little boys stand up very straight, raising their lanterns above their heads. The girl is looking at the ceiling. She is really quite fat, her podgy face expressionless, her thick ankles visible below the hem of the improvised white dress. The song-books are ring-binders decorated with cut-out pictures and the words 'Christmas Joy'. Almost in unison the binders open. Almost in unison the carol-singers lower their eyes, stop beaming and start to sing.

The first song is one of their own. A little man in a faded fair-isle waistcoat bangs out the rhythm, making the metal bells of the tambourine rattle and clash. At certain moments he raises it to shoulder height for extra emphasis. The woman with the satin blouse has the zither on the table in front of her. She slides her hands across it, making broken chords with her thumb, then quieting the vibration with her fingers. She is so accomplished she can make eye contact with her audience at the same time. She can play and sing and beam all at once. Still smiling, she pushes her full lips out and forwards; she can make every little word count.

The old people make no attempt to join in. The tune is unfamiliar to them, and most of the words, too. And they are sleepy after their lunch. Fran in the corner is too far gone even to notice. Rodney looks up at the strangers and gives a sour grunt. Bessie calls out, 'I love yer,' as usual. She looks across at the woman in the satin blouse and calls out, 'Ow, I love yer. Good boy, y're a good boy. Come 'ere!'

But the next song is one they all know better, an old tune the residents half-remember from childhood. Only the words are strange. One or two of them smile in recognition, or even tap their feet. In the transparent bags taped to their legs the urine shivers. Only the words are different and confusing. They look at the zither woman for help and she sings with extra verve, the light playing on the cream satin of her blouse as it strains and deflates with her breathing. They look in her direction and she enfolds them all in her beam.

Sister Manning has shrunk slightly farther inside the kitchen doorway. The woman in the blouse extends her full lips, enunciates every word clearly, so it can be heard even in the farthest corners of the room. 'We who halting are and slow... ' she sings, pulling and stretching her mouth as if she were speaking to the deaf, each word a little elastic feat. The accompanying singers slow their pace to match the words, as if by previous arrangement. Even the tambourine man has altered his tempo smoothly to match hers. And then for a moment the music stops and she repeats the words without singing them. '*We... who... halting... are... and slow...*' she says, accentuating each word. 'That's *you*, brothers and sisters. *You* are slow, *you* are halting. And God loves you particularly. And this Christmas He has sent down His son, His only son, to die for *you*, to save *you*. So even if you're slow, you don't have to worry!' She looks at Fran, collapsed in her chair, the square hole of her mouth fallen wide open. 'Even if you're halting, you can still be full of Joy this Christmastide. Because Jesus has come for you! He's come to save you!'

'Ow, y're a good boy!' Bessie shouts. 'Ow, I love yer, I love yer!'

The woman looks down at her satin bosom, pulling in her chin. She draws her fingers across the strings in a lingering chord. She looks across at Bessie and beams. Eleven hands turn eleven pages, and the singing starts up again.

From where Reg is sitting the music is almost deafening. He's as close to the singing as the singers are to one another, the repeated clash and clink of the tambourine sounding almost inside his ear.

The big-busted woman in the cream satin stands right over him, the shiny wrinkles of cloth coming and going under her armpit. Her lower lip pouts and stretches in time to the tambourine. The music's so loud that at first he can hardly hear it. It could be an old silent film he's watching, a film that flickers in pale satin to a crash of unrelated sound.

But then something changes. That tune... Isn't it something he remembers from way back? An old song from the War, something lovers used to hear in their heads as they said goodbye. Didn't he hear it at the Regal once, with Margaret, in '39, right at the beginning? He strains to catch the words, but they don't seem to come in the right places, the beat's all wrong. But it *is* the same song; he still remembers. Behind the man with the grin the lights of the Christmas-tree blur, the little coloured stars softly expand against the dark green.

In a moment Gemma's at his elbow. She's kneeling beside him in her pale blue uniform, her hand on his shoulder. 'Reg,' she's saying to him. 'What's the matter? What is it, darling? Give me your hanky.'

He lets her feel for it in his pockets and then give it to him to mop his own eyes with. His face seems to be all wet. He rubs the crumpled hanky over his cheeks, his chin. He blots his eyes with it. He holds it next to his right eye in case he needs to start crying again.

At the side of his chair he can feel Gemma's soft bulk, her warmth through the pale blue cloth. She's a sweet girl. She says, 'Are you too close here, Reg? Shall I move you, darling?' He likes it when she calls him darling. No one really calls him darling, since Margaret. And Margaret doesn't seem to come and see him much these days. 'Reg?' Gemma says.

When she speaks she leans in closer to him to catch what he's saying. 'No. No.' How can he make his voice loud enough over the noise of the tambourine? She mustn't move him, mustn't take him away from the lovely old songs. But he can't seem to manage much more than a whisper. 'Leave me here. I'm all right here,' he says. She mustn't take him away from the tune he sang with Margaret and the woman with the satin blouse that ripples like water over her breast, sending little spidery streaks of light up under her arm.

But the music's broken off now and there's only the woman talking. She seems to be telling him something about his family. How can she know his family? How can she even have met his brothers and sisters, when they live so far away now? Even his mother hardly ever manages to come and visit him any more.

The carol-singers have moved away from the Christmas-tree. They're going round the room, leaning over Rodney, leaning over Fran, shaking all the hands one by one. 'God be with you,' they're saying. 'Jesus is born again.' Is it possible to be born more than once? When Lily was born his mother made those noises from the upstairs room. It sounded dreadful, like an animal. Would you want it all to happen twice? Would you still want all those brothers and sisters, the kitchen full of little brothers and sisters, the blacked range shining under its pot of mutton stew? Perhaps if they were born again they'd come and see him. Perhaps even Margaret would come, if she could just hear the song.

He's the last one they get to. The man with the black smile leans over him. 'Peace be with you, brother,' he says. He picks up Reg's hand where it lies in his lap and shakes it.

The woman with the shiny blouse is there too. When she bends down to him the light over her breasts comes and goes. 'Jesus is come for *you*, brother,' she says.

He struggles to pull himself forward in his chair so that he can speak to her. 'That song...' he says. 'You know, in '39, my wife...'

But she doesn't seem to hear him. She's not like Gemma. She doesn't even seem to be listening. 'Peace be with you, brother,' she says and moves on.

And now they're back in their places by the tree. He's at the woman's right hand. And the wonderful music is starting up again. The two boys have moved forward. They take up their position, one on either side of the space left by the horseshoe of chairs. They raise their lanterns high, standing very still.

And the little girl comes into the centre, a sweet fair thing in a circle of light. She stands on tiptoe and raises her arms, and her white translucent wings unfold from the very tips of her fingers, reaching almost to the ground. As the carol-singers lift up their voices, she turns slowly, the glow from the lanterns falling on her hair, glinting in the soft ring of silver fur she wears for a crown. He dabs his eyes again. She's turning and turning, lifting her dainty feet, taking a few frail steps to one side and then to the other, half-running to where he is. 'Ow, y're lovely. Let me see yer. Good boy, good boy!' He hears Bessie's voice as if it were coming from the inside of his own head, as if it were his own. *Oh, Margaret. Let me see yer. Y're a good boy.* She's an angel. She turns on tiptoe, her lacy wings wide open. She's everything, all his sisters, all the family he needs.

She sinks to the floor, her head bent in the soft light of the lanterns, her wings folded round her like a mist. One by one, the ring-binders of carols are closing quietly. 'Christmas Joy,' they say. 'Christmas Joy.' The boys shuffle from one foot to the other and the man in the fair-isle jersey unhooks the lanterns from their poles and sets them down on the table side by side. He picks up the two sticks and tucks them under his arm. The woman with the red plaits goes over to the girl and unfastens her wings. She's rolling them up and putting them away. The man with the dark smile gathers up the instruments. Sister Manning's come forward out of the kitchen doorway. And the singers are leaving. They're saying, 'God bless you, sister.' And Sister Manning's helping them to get their things together, ushering them out of the lounge and into the front hall. Reg presses the handkerchief against his cheek. He'll have to remember it all to tell Margaret when she comes. He feels a draught as the outer door opens. Over the television the foil garlands twinkle and sway.

How

How she'd loved Paul then more than anyone or anything in the world. How she still loved him. How now it was just more mature and realistic and sensible. Not a compromise, exactly, but all the same you had to be able to function. How they hadn't known each other that long at that point and she'd been completely crazy. How she was just a child really, even as a graduate student, even at twenty-three. How she was so much in love with Paul she didn't know what she was doing. How she wasn't capable of seeing anyone or anything but him.

How that was what it was like to live hundreds of miles apart. How she'd arrived once at his bedsit in Leeds and sat there on the floor in the dark, weeping. How when he came back he almost tripped over her. How he picked her up in his arms. How that night they lay together like spoons in his single bed and she thought this was all she could imagine ever wanting. How the next morning she'd had to hide from the landlord, peeing into a yoghurt-pot so as not to give herself away. How they put on Pink Floyd and Paul walked round the room naked, conducting. How they'd existed on nothing but takeaways and withered apples. How he dared her to lean out of the dormer window and drop her core on someone's head, and she did it. How she can still hear his approving laugh.

How when she was back in Brighton and the tall thin boy from Malawi asked her out it somehow didn't even occur to her to say no. How it couldn't possibly do any harm to anyone. How at this distance she has trouble even remembering what he was like – it's as if all the details have been wiped out. How at this point she doesn't even remember his name.

How she'd said yes because she didn't want to hurt his feelings. How he was in a foreign country, alone, and she knew what loneliness was. How he had that smile, those amazing teeth. How she must have been feeling generous. How she didn't want to be the sort of girl she knew she was really, the sort that would look into that big smile and just say no.

How he came to pick her up at Woodlands. How she was in her old jeans and T-shirt – no point dressing up. How she'd even told him about Paul – though, looking back, she can see she didn't say it in the right tone, didn't say it emphatically enough. How it would have seemed rude to insist – you didn't want to make him feel he was somehow second best. How he was so excited about everything! How they took the bus into town because he said he got such a kick out of the double-decker buses. How they went upstairs to sit at the front on the top deck and he was almost beside himself with excitement. How she tries to remember his voice, and fails completely. How for a moment she just catches the curve of his long fingers and the sudden flash of his smile.

How when he told her the film he'd chosen was *Naughty Knickers* she hadn't immediately slapped him or run out. How she'd thought it didn't matter, this was how they did things in Malawi, he was lonely. How she didn't want to make him feel small, or clumsy, or inadequate. How she sat through two excruciating hours in complete silence, hardly seeing the screen at all. How all she remembers now is a vague succession of body-parts, and the effort of keeping her face expressionless, the almost overwhelming urge to laugh.

Yet how, when they got back to Woodlands, it had seemed quite natural to ask him up to her room. How she'd made him coffee. How they sat side by side on the bed and he put his arm round her, his fingers dangling next to her breast. How she hadn't dared ask him all about his life in

Malawi, how she was afraid of her own ignorance, afraid of being laughed at. How she let him kiss her because she felt ashamed – it seemed the least she could do. How somehow she found herself half-undressed with him on the single bed and she panicked, she thought, *What am I doing?* How she pulled away from him and sat up in the half-dark and covered her face with her hands.

How now she can see she got off quite lightly. How she ended up sucking him off because she owed him at least that much. How from here she remembers nothing – not what he looked like with his eyes shut, or whether the noises he made were the same as Paul's, or if he went to sleep afterwards, or stroked her face.

How a few days later, when she caught sight of him in the refectory in a group of African students, she carried her food to a table over on the other side, where she couldn't see them. How when she took her tray back he came up behind her and said something in her ear – what was it, something about English girls, they were so cheap and stupid, letting themselves be fucked by anyone, a complete waste of time.

How she'd said nothing. How she put down her tray on top of the pile and slipped out through the side door, past the launderette, past the bookshop, towards a clump of bushes. How she crouched down and threw up into a mess of – what was it? – rhododendrons. How she doesn't even remember his name. How she was in love with Paul then, and she's never told Paul any of it. How now she's much more mature and sensible, and anyway what would have been the point?

How after all these years she finds herself lying awake in the dark and thinking, *What* was *his life like back in Malawi? What did he care about, what did he really want?* How somehow at this distance she feels certain there was someone else. How he must have had a girl at home who was missing him, who lay night after night conjuring his face in the darkness, hearing his voice in her head.

How perhaps they've actually stayed together. How they're probably married now, like her and Paul, only they've got a whole family of children with those same long fingers, that same grin. How the mother's wearing a leaf-print dress in shades of green and orange, cooking something with plantains in a big pot. How she stands straight-backed, her hand on her hip. How she stops stirring for a moment and raises her deep brown eyes.

-

Cave

It doesn't surprise her that he's late. She sits waiting with a glossy magazine on her knees, turning over the pages of advertisements almost without seeing them – stick-women in black, in feathers, with fake beauty-spots, with eyeshadow that covers almost the whole socket. Letters, horoscopes, holidays in the Bahamas, in rural France. And there, tucked away in a corner where hardly anyone would see it, a small photograph of a cave-painting, shadowy red shapes of animals leaping on dark rock.

When he finally comes up the stairs he's panting. He nods at her and goes past her into his room. She can hear something creaking, the small rustle and click as he hangs up his coat, the rattle of drawers, other little noises she has no way of interpreting. After a moment he opens the door again and calls her in.

Already he's starting to apologise, his round cheeks shining. He's still agitated – still breathing fast, his hands flying about as he talks, busy at the computer. 'That traffic!

It's unbelievable! Right from the industrial estate, have you seen it lately? I was all right till I got off the by-pass, but then it was all snarled up, everything at a standstill. I knew I had you coming in at nine. But all I could do was just sit there. And I thought I'd left plenty of time. And I had. Plenty! If it hadn't been for the traffic,' he says.

She sits in the black chair, watching him. Little strands of hair have come adrift from his red bald crown and dangle down beside his ears. His mouth still pours out excuses. His grey pullover has ridden up around his waist in a soft spare tyre. His feet, side by side on the blue floor, look somehow larger than they ought to be. She says, 'They do say it's been getting worse.'

'Anyway.' In the pale light from the window his nose is red. 'What are we doing for you this morning? A lens check, is it?' He goes quiet for a moment, reading her notes. He looks up at her and says, 'You were in America two years ago, I see.'

'Yes.'

'In Washington? Did you get to see Washington?'

She shakes her head.

'I've got a daughter in Washington – political researcher. What do you think of that?'

She opens her mouth to answer.

'Wonderful job she's got. Wonderful. And in...' – he looks at his watch – '...approximately three and a half hours from now she'll be on that phone, contacting all sorts of people, getting her first camera-crew together. Can you believe it? First time she's ever had to do that. Quite a responsibility.' He runs his tongue over his lips. 'I keep thinking of her. All that to cope with, at her age. Imagine. Only twenty-six, and all those people looking to her already. Can you even begin to wrap your mind round that?'

'I don't know,' she says. He's examining her lenses now, flashing his little light in her eyes in the darkened room. Her chin is thrust forward, on the black rest. She blinks. She looks up, to the left, to the right. She blinks. She looks down, and he gently lifts her eyelid, his face so close to hers she can see the pores in his skin, feel his breath on her cheek.

'Well, that all looks fine,' he says. 'What about Yosemite? You ever been there?'

'No, I—'

'Let me tell you about Yosemite!' he says. 'The great wide open spaces!' He makes a sound that's something like a snort. 'When we got to Yosemite they had a "full up" notice on the gates. Can't you just see it?'

She shakes her head.

'Full up, I ask you! That's what we go to the States to get away from! And Big Sur! You ever been to Big Sur?'

She grunts. She can't move her head now, the black frame-thing across the top of her face and each lens dropping down in front of her eye, replaced quickly by another.

'This one?' he says. 'Or this one?' Her first clear view of the letters on the wall is snatched away. He goes back to it. 'Or this?' He alternates the first with a third and she doesn't answer, unable to decide. 'Let me tell you something about Big Sur!' he says. She blinks. Her eyes are watering. Furtively she brushes the drop of water away with her finger. 'This little seat up on the cliff,' he's saying. 'The solitary view-point where you're supposed to sit and be moved by the awesome landscape, man against the elements, man in his naked state? The one they take all the photos from? Completely overrun with tourists! Crawling! Coaches and coaches of them. That lovely coastline – you've seen the pictures. He raises the shutter over her other eye. He clicks his tongue. 'Well, your prescription doesn't seem to change much, anyway. Can you read the letters for me, right down to the bottom?' She reads them, the little shapes small but clear, infinitely removed from where she is, but somehow still legible, somehow still recognisable as something she's almost always known.

He pulls the black frame back, away from her face. She sits forward, ready to stand up. 'Did you let your G.P. know about that trouble you had last time you were in the

160

U.S.?' he asks her. 'It was a lens incident, we decided. Not an eye incident. But all the same... I hope you went and saw him. I hope you told him what happened.'

She shakes her head. 'No, I... It didn't seem necessary.'

He's frowning. She can just make out his frown in the half-darkness. 'What was it that American eye-doctor told you?'

'Nothing much. He wanted to do more tests. I told him not to bother.'

Her optician laughs. 'Tell me about it!' he says. 'It's like that over there. They're so afraid of litigation they'll put you through anything. They'd sew up your eyelids if that's what it took to cover their backs. My daughter tells me. It'd make your hair stand on end, some of it. And it's happening all the time.' He looks at his watch. 'She's asleep now, of course. She won't be waking up for another couple of hours yet.'

'It's a big day,' she says. 'Exciting. You must be really proud of her. It must be quite exciting for *you*.'

He's still bent over her notes, half-crouched at his desk, his face lit from underneath in the gleam of the little child's desk-lamp he uses. He looks half mad, the shadows in the wrong places, his sweating face a comic devil's, or a clown's. He swivels on his chair and turns towards her again. Something's bothering him. 'Just one thing before you go. Let me just take one last look.'

She sits obediently as he comes to her again, flashing his little silver torch in her eyes. The light seems to reach into her brain and touch something. When he takes it away she can see the blood-vessels outlined on red like bare trees, an after-image of her own retina. She blinks. When she opens her eyes again the image still remains for a moment.

He examines her eyes for what seems a long time, his face almost touching hers, his own eye almost unblinking, huge to her as he peers into hers as if into a cave. Finally he sits back in his chair. 'Mmm,' he says. He swivels his chair to the desk. He writes something in her notes, turns back again to face her. 'The backs of your eyes are an odd shape,' he tells her. 'Most people's are cupped.' He puts down the little torch and makes a bowl of his two hands to show her. 'But yours are quite flat. Quite healthy, otherwise. As far as I can see, anyway. I'm sure it's nothing. Some people just have flatter eyes than others. Some people are taller than others. Some people have pointed noses... It's almost certainly just the way your eyes naturally are. And I'm only doing a lens check. They're fine. Everything's fine.' He's folding her notes and putting them back in their cardboard envelope. 'Of course, in someone else...' he says, smiling. 'In someone else it could always be the start of some... neurological disorder.' He gives a little hiccup that could be embarrassment, or laughter, his face in the circle of light redder now even than it was at the beginning. And she is smiling with him, in spite of herself.

'What kind of... neurological disorder?'

'Don't ask,' he says. 'You don't want to know. It's something that fortunately we don't even have to think about.' He's still grinning at her, his face shining under what seem to be little beads of sweat. With embarrassment, probably. Wishing he hadn't started this. He needs a strong cup of coffee to pick him up, get him over the hump, smooth over all that business with the traffic and the guilt and the apologies, the way the whole day started out completely on the wrong foot. In Washington it's still only 4.30 a.m. His daughter's turning over in bed, burying her head in the pillow to muffle the buzz of the air-conditioning, the sounds of the city below her, the sirens. She's still got a few hours before she has to surface and pick up the telephone, dial the numbers in her Filofax for camera, sound, lighting, continuity.

He's standing up now. He draws back the curtain and the little room's suddenly flooded with sunlight. She picks up her bag and pulls on her jacket awkwardly. At the door she turns back to him. She looks him right in the eye as she says, 'Do you mind if I ask you something?'

'Of course not. Ask away.'

She hesitates for a moment, waits until he's starting to look uncomfortable. Then she says, 'Would it be all right if I nicked your magazine?'

For a moment he doesn't understand her. 'Magazine?'

'The one I was reading before you called me in?'

'Oh, do. Do.' His head jerks towards the chair where the glossy pages still lie open, face downwards.

'Thanks.' She scoops it up as she goes past. 'For everything. I hope your daughter has a really terrific day.'

She sits on her own at the café table, stirring her coffee to a spinning blur. Beside her cup, the magazine lies open where she left it, the dark photograph of the cave in the corner, the reddish shapes of animals stretching their running arch over the wall of rock. At Yosemite the gates are locked for the night. At Big Sur a mist sweeps in from the Pacific, blotting out everything. Her eyes are tired. She wills herself to focus on the caption, to read the small print of the article itself. No longer open to tourists, it says. These days all you can get to see is a replica. Not the thing itself. She looks hard at the photo. Is it a reproduction of the replica, or of the real cave paintings? It's impossible to tell. Is the arc of the beast's spine and front legs too perfect? Is the terracotta glow across its flanks too bright?

In her mind's eye she's trying to catch something. What is it exactly? A deer? A bison? Something that's become extinct? And she imagines it in a hundred years' time, in two hundred, a thousand – a deer, a whole frieze, a running herd of deer, surviving perfectly in that darkness, picked out suddenly by a single probing torch-beam, glowing on in the dark when the beam goes out. There's a fire smoking in the cave-mouth, fat dripping into the flames, the scraped hides hanging. A rocky shelf of flints, in different shapes and sizes, the deep dark bowl of the cave itself, the barely curving surfaces where the paintings are. A moving beam picks out forelegs, head, spine, haunches. And another, the design repeated almost exactly. And then the torch goes out – a sudden dark hand closes over the transparent plastic, light escaping like blood from between the dark fingers. She looks at her watch. In Washington it's 7 a.m precisely. She sees the leaping animals run on.

Success

i.m. Lewis Nordan

You'd have to be a student or desperate to want to travel up North by coach. And I was too old now to be a student – well past the rucksack and bare midriff stage. I made myself small in my pathetic little window corner. There was just enough of a ledge to rest my elbow on and I put my chin in my hand. It was taking a long time to shake free of Victoria. Around us the taxis nosed and revved and hooted. We were stuck like a dead beetle in an anthill. And, as if that wasn't enough, the guy next to me had a ventriloquist's dummy sitting on his knee.

I tried not to turn and look. After a while Victoria gave way to Paddington and then to Kilburn. In a minute we'd finally be crossing the North Circular. Around me the other passengers were talking and exchanging jokes. Across the aisle an older woman opened a packet of sandwiches, and the whole coach started to stink of eggs. Then the buildings began to space themselves out and spikes of dusty buddleia waved in the gaps. The city was sucked back somewhere behind us as the traffic noises settled to a steady hum. 'Are you going on holiday?' a voice said.

I turned and looked at the man in the aisle seat next to mine. As far as I could tell he hadn't said anything. 'I'm sorry?'

He was a small man with receding hair and a blotchy complexion. He shook his head as he looked at me. His mouth didn't move. 'I do like to be beside the seaside,' the voice said.

I looked down at the dummy. I'd never had the chance to see one close up. It was about the size of a six-year-old kid, moulded out of something hard and man-made in an unlikely clear pink. Someone had decided to dress it like a small snooker player, in a violet silk shirt and black bow tie. The black satin waistcoat had the word 'Victor' embroidered across it in purple. The thing sat on the man's lap stiffly, its jointed legs sticking out so its knees touched the seat in front. As I stared, its mouth fell open suddenly. Its eyes rolled. 'No good looking at Ron,' it said. 'Miserable bastard, Ron is. Says nought to anyone if he can help it. Won't even give you the time of day.'

I smiled in spite of myself. 'Is that right?'

'Just as well he's got me to speak up for him. Get sweet Fanny Adams out of him otherwise.'

The mouth was mesmerising. It reminded me of the polystyrene carton round a Big Mac. I turned my back and tried to look out of the window again. We were on the M1. A sign whipped past, flashing Hemel Hempstead, St. Albans. Beyond, a sliproad, a suggestion of roundabout, a queue of waiting traffic across a bridge. Above us the sky was full of rainclouds, a low grey ceiling. *Tiddly-om-pom-pom*, a voice in my head sang.

The movement of the coach was rocking me gently. I pressed the recliner button and closed my eyes. Through the rising hum of the engine I could still hear the woman across the aisle talking to her neighbour. A few words, and then I lost her, thank God, as the driver changed down to take a hill. '...With a lace bodice...' The phrase drifted over me. '...What to give the bridesmaids...' she said. Banging on about some wedding. Was that all they could manage? *Where the brass band plays.* I moved my head slightly so my open hand covered my left ear.

I jumped. The thing next to me was talking to me again. 'I bet you're wondering what sort of bloke Ron is.'

Oh yeah? I turned to look at them both. The shutter over its eye closed and opened again in a mechanical wink. I stared into Ron's eyes. 'He should be so lucky,' I said.

'*Aw...*' The thing half keeled over on Ron's lap with disappointment. 'Don't be like that. Here we are, two handsome lads on the road together, both unattached. And an attractive young lady like yourself...'

'I'm not a young lady,' I said.

The McMouth shook in what was obviously meant to be a laugh. 'Come on,' it said. 'Ron's not such a bad bloke. Cross my heart. You'd like him. And successful with it!'

It was hard to keep my voice level. 'Is he,' I said.

'Successful? He's bloody fantastic! You should see him. Gets them going every time. Laugh! You should hear them! No one to touch him in the whole bloody North-East!'

'Good for Ron,' I said.

'Booked solid now right up to the end of October. Can't get us for love nor money.'

'Is that right.'

'He's a bloody marvel, you know that? It's not every day you find yourself sat next to someone like him.'

'No,' I said. 'He's the first bloody marvel I've come across.'

'And he doesn't even drink!' I felt the dummy bounce up and down on the man's knees. In the window I saw its reflection twist its head theatrically to look at me. 'Won't touch the stuff. Never has. Not if I can help it. Never see *him* come out pub at closing-time and fall int' gutter like a stuck pig. And don't let them tell you owt different. Bloody liars, all of them!' I heard it close its mouth with a snap.

170

Something was jabbing me in the ribs. I dragged my eyes from the grey-green blur at the window and turned to look properly. Its hair was standing on end over one ear. 'Well, have you?' it said.

'What?'

'Have you ever seen him have one over the eight? Go on, be honest. You can say what you like to me.'

I looked at the man hard. His lips still hadn't moved. His nose was like an old cigar-butt, squashed sideways, dark with creases. 'No,' I said.

The dummy sat back on the man's lap with a little satisfied jerk. 'You've heard of him, though, eh? Ron Burfield. He's a household name, almost. Anywhere north of Luton he's the first name springs to mind. You couldn't not have heard of him. You'd have to have been out of the country or in a bloody coma. Or living in a box.'

'You would,' I said. I thought of my own life, in which Ron Burfield had not so far figured. I thought of its cardboard sides and the brown tape that sealed the joins. I thought of its dimensions, and the polystyrene nuggets that filled out the corners, the address scrawled on the outside in felt tip. I thought of the tiny holes the light came through, the nauseating lurches when someone picked the box up and tilted it unthinkingly from side to side. *Tiddly-om-pom-pom.* Next to me the dummy was quiet, almost limp. Its mauve silk shirt gleamed under the passing lights. I turned and looked it in its painted eye. 'So tell me,' I said. 'What's the secret of your friend's world-shattering success?'

On the other side of the glass the rain had started properly now. Our tyres made a swishing sound on the surface of the road. I leaned in towards the centre aisle and craned my neck to see where we were going. Spray slapped the windscreen and was pushed to one side by the single wiper and streamed back. We were following a cloud. Inside it I could just make out the dark shape of a lorry. I sank back in my seat and closed my eyes again.

The coach swayed on its wheels. It was a godawful old crate, shuddering with noises. Among them I thought I could hear voices I recognised. Then the sound of glass breaking, something running down the far wall. I screwed my eyes tight shut and burrowed into the scratchy plush of the seat-back. *Oh I do like to walk along the prom prom prom.* The fucking pillow was making the side of my face sore.

I rubbed my hands over the seat. Relax, I told myself. It's a load of shit. Forget it. I was miles away already, I'd left it all behind, it didn't matter. This time the voice I heard came from the seat behind me – an old man's. 'That's a good job he's got now,' he was saying. I heard the wife mumble something in agreement. 'Good money, holiday in Tenerife, new Ford Focus. What more could you ask for?' Again the woman's voice said something I couldn't catch. 'Oh, they're all right,' the man said to her. 'She'll come round. No damage done.' I opened my left eye a slit and watched the grey-green fields streaking away under the grey sky.

The stupid dummy hadn't answered my question. It looked completely gormless, slumped on the man's lap. I poked it in its hard stomach and it jerked upright. 'You were going to tell me about Ron,' I said. 'How he manages to be so rich and famous. And not sell out to the lifestyle. He must be severely tempted.' I looked at Ron. His face didn't twitch but his eyes twinkled. His suit was old and shiny. The outdated lapels curled slightly. It looked as if it hadn't been cleaned in years. I turned and faced him directly. 'It's just a trick, right? Anyone can throw their voice if they know how.'

The dummy's face snapped open and shut again. 'No use asking him,' it said. 'He's a close bastard. He won't give anything away. But there's no magic, you can take it from me. You keep your mouth shut and let someone else do the talking, it's as easy as that. Think what you want to say and who's going to say it, and where they're sat. And project it into them. You just have to make sure your lips don't move.'

'Oik iss,' I said.

The mouth clapped open and shut several times in quick succession. It was laughing at me again. 'Is that the best you can do?' it said. As I watched, Ron Burfield slid a small flat bottle out of his pocket and unscrewed the cap. He drank from it directly and wiped his lips on the back of his hand. The McMouth let out a long shuddering 'Aaaah!' Ron held up the bottle and offered it to me, but I shook my head. 'Let me have another go,' I said.

For a few miles I tried for myself, silently. A couple of rows in front of us a little girl was playing with a doll. She twirled it so its filmy dress flew out in a circle. She stroked and patted and re-parted its stiff hair, talking to it all the time in a soft voice. Once the doll lost a shoe and the little girl slid to the floor and grovelled under the seat until she found it and put it back on. She held the doll horizontal and moved its long thin plastic legs so it walked up the window-pane. Then she walked it back down. A moment later the doll appeared above her head-rest, bowing and twirling. I threw my voice to the doll but nothing happened. The doll refused to utter a single word. I could feel my own mouth move, like I was chewing. And the words I'd been thinking were unspoken and simple and sad.

I must have drifted off to sleep. I was somewhere else, somewhere miles from there, and dreaming. I was a girl of seventeen, all her life ahead of her, just starting out. I was going to University, first term, in jeans and a threadbare sweater I hadn't worn for yonks. On the seat beside me was my back-pack, its straps dark with sweat. My fifty-year-old parents stood at the kerb to watch as we drew away, four outstretched arms waving me goodbye.

I hadn't done anything yet. I hadn't learnt anything, or lived away from home, or met any of the people I'd live with. I'd barely even slept with anyone. I hadn't tasted tacos or snails or tobacco or retsina. I'd never opened a bottle of wine. I hadn't read a non-fiction book. I hadn't learnt to speak Italian or balance a bank-statement, or insert a tampon. I didn't know how it felt to own a car or lose a parent or have a child or get divorced. I hardly knew how it felt to fail.

I opened my eyes. Beside me Ron Burfield was asleep with his mouth open, snoring gently, his narrow chest rising and falling in a fume of whisky, the stale smell of him so warm and thick that for a moment I almost gagged. Victor seemed to be asleep too, though his eyes were still open. He stared straight ahead, at the little disposable paper cloth over the back of the seat in front. I could see the roots of his nylon hair, the vertical lines where his mouth opened, the slit at the back of his clothes where the man's hand went in. I thought of the little girl and the doll. I could hear the girl's voice gently rising and falling, and the little click of its feet against the window. I strained to hear the tune.

And then suddenly I was doing it! Quite clearly I heard the child's voice say, 'She's a wonderful dancer. She can dance all up and down the glass.' It was astonishing. My lips hadn't moved at all. With all the power I could muster I concentrated on the woman across the aisle. 'They were so happy,' I heard her say. 'As they came out into the porch you could see it in their faces. They were just potty about each other. No one could have been more in love.'

What was happening? I felt myself starting to shake. I shifted my attention from the woman and projected it onto the man behind me. 'So good at that job...' he said. 'Look at what he's built up just in those few years. Can you imagine what they'd do without him now if he was to leave?'

I reached out and poked the dummy but its eyes didn't move. I heard the little girl say, 'She twirled and twirled and her skirt flew out around her like petals.' She was silent for a moment. Then she corrected herself. 'Like a rainbow.' *A rainbow, tiddly-om?* 'Like the sun,' she said. I rubbed at the condensation with my sleeve. On the other side of the glass it was still raining. As we passed a bus-stop the queueing umbrellas brushed along our flank like a stream of balloons.

Baby

When the ambulance drops her in front of her block of flats, she hardly dares to climb out, the white bundle in her arms seems so small and fragile. She sits shivering with cold or nervousness, clutching it to her shoulder, until the driver opens the rear doors and comes to help her down. He touches her elbow gently and guides her to the front door. Together they cross the echoing concrete stairwell scrawled with graffiti to where the lift stands open, its metal doors gaping. As they travel upwards to her floor, he leans over and strokes back a little wisp of hair from the baby's forehead.

'You'll be all right, love?' He looks at her almost paternally as he puts down her battered holdall and backs towards the landing.

'Yeah.' She can tell he's sorry for her. He gets called out here quite often – on Saturday nights, especially, after the pubs throw out. 'It's all right,' she says. 'We'll be okay.

I've been here two months already. He'll have his own room and everything. It's not like it's a squat.'

'No.' He laughs, but it sounds slightly uneasy. 'I believe you. Thousands wouldn't.' He hesitates. 'Anyway, you know where to find us. You've got the phone number. I don't have to tell you where we are.'

When he's gone she goes into the room she thinks of as the baby's bedroom and unwraps him carefully, cradling the back of his head in her hand. She lays him down on the plastic mat and starts to change his nappy. She's not used to it yet, she doesn't seem to have enough hands, but he's a good baby, he hardly even wriggles. She puts him down in the borrowed crib, his little cheek squashed into the mattress, his mouth pushed out of shape so he looks almost cross. For a few seconds she stands staring down at him, listening to his light breathing, watching the folds of the blanket rise and fall. He's so tiny. At a sudden loud noise from outside – a motor-bike revving, someone shouting something – he jumps, throwing his head back and his arms out to either side. He gives a little whine of protest, then settles back into his dream, sucking noisily on his closed fist. The soft breathing starts up again. She's almost frightened it'll stop if she tiptoes away too soon.

*

All that first day he does nothing but sleep. She hears sounds under her – doors slamming, the clatter of feet, loud laughter echoing in the stairwell, the clank and crash of the lift. But in his crib her baby hardly stirs. It's not until the night-time that he starts to wake up properly, looking at her out of those big unfocused eyes of his and rooting for her nipple through the crumpled, milky fabric of her clothes. Whimpering, then crying. Then screaming, his face flushed with what seems to her like anger, long shuddering breaths of pure noise.

But when she's feeding him, his mouth clamped to her breast, he looks so contented. She settles back on the low chair and hears nothing but the rhythmic murmur of his satisfaction, sees nothing but the gentle filling and emptying of his cheeks, the tiny pulse beating in the top of his soft head. Outside, just sky, the usual haze of the city. The roar of a late car, silence, a door-slam, and it squeals away. And in here just the two of them. She could almost swear her baby's growing, a bit less frail already, a bit plumper than he was – that she's already given him some part of herself he needed. In a few months he'll look like one of those advertisement photos, a cuddly one-year-old standing in nothing but a disposable nappy, looking back at her upside-down from the space between his fat thighs.

*

The days pass, all alike, and she doesn't see anyone. There are only sounds. People laughing in the stairwell, drunken singing. Cars that come and go. Once, the sharp sounds of a quarrel, a man's voice shouting, 'You fucking bitch!', slurring the syllables. Then a woman screaming, subsiding in a confusion of choking sobs. In the dark of the early morning, the faint whirr of a milk-float, a long way down.

And the nights are alike too. The baby wakes at ten, and again at two. Sometimes after she's fed him he refuses to go down again. If she tries to put him back in the crib his body starts to tense up and go red, his arms and legs working. His little mouth opens on a round O of silence as she waits for the first shriek. She picks him up hurriedly and he looks back at her, calm and alert. She unbuttons herself again and he pats her skin gently with his open fingers, dragging on her empty breast until she closes her eyes and the tears squeeze out from under her eyelids on to his soft hair.

And he's doing well, she only has to look at him. His cheeks have lost that wizened look. His fingers aren't as long and thin as they were. He's losing the frog-belly and little out-turned frog-legs of a newborn and plumping up. When she fastens the tabs of his nappy she could swear she's having to pull harder to make the two sides meet.

*

One night he wakes her at four. It feels as if she hasn't even had time to drop off. She struggles to open her eyes. But his crying's a kind of frenzy that reaches into the deepest part of her body – she doesn't have any alternative. She sits up in the near-darkness, the walls of the bedroom reeling, and puts her bare feet to the floor. She goes into his room and picks him up. He flops against her shoulder and stops crying. She can feel his damp cheek against hers, the little hairless patch on the top of his head where he's rubbed himself almost bald on the end of the crib. What's the matter with him? She tries to dredge up what people have told her about babies, so she'll know what to expect. She undoes her nightdress. Both her nipples are sore and cracked from the way he pulls at them. As he takes her in his mouth, she almost cries out.

When she's fed him, she sits and holds him for a minute in her arms, feeling the warm, heavy weight of him in her lap. He belches and a little stream of milk runs down into the creases of his neck. Somewhere out in the alley, the snarl of a couple of fighting cats. And then a liquid rumble, quite close. Her baby is filling his nappy. His face has gone purple. After a while, she lays him down on the changing mat and starts to take off his clothes.

Everything's soaked with a pale, mustard-coloured mess. The nappy's full of it – soft and wet and slightly granular. His legs are coated, and the legs of the Babygro.

He's got shit between his toes. The shawl's marked with a jagged stain. Even the skirt of her dressing-gown is soaked yellow where he was sitting on her knees. She scrapes the curds off into the toilet, puts the clothes all to soak in a bucket, grabs a clean nappy. But when she goes to do up the tab, the back and front won't come together. She pulls and pulls, but there's still half an inch of softly bulging flesh that won't let itself be covered. The baby's fat thighs fill out the leg-holes completely, ringed with pink where the plastic's starting to cut in. In the end she gives up and wraps him in an old-fashioned towelling nappy she's dug out from the back of the cupboard. Tomorrow she'll go out and get him the next size up. She didn't realise they grew so fast. Nobody ever told her these things. As she leans over the crib to put him back into it he opens his eyes and looks at her sleepily. He pulls up the corners of his mouth in what must be his first smile.

The next morning she dresses him up in cosy-toes and woolly hat and mittens and carries him to the lift with the buggy. At the bottom the doors clank open on a small huddle of young girls. They turn their backs on her, giggling in a fog of smoke. She catches them glancing back at her over their shoulders, laughing even harder. She doesn't look at them. She unfolds the buggy and straps him into it. As she pushes it towards the door the girls step aside to make room. She catches the words 'little fat pig' as she goes past.

She leaves the estate quickly, crossing the open grass by a path that cuts diagonally towards the shopping arcade. Strewn across the ground, wads of crumpled kitchen paper and broken polystyrene trays shiver in the wind as she steers between them. By the time she reaches the chemist's, a few drops of cold rain have fallen on her arms, making dark spots on the sleeves of her jacket. She picks up a packet of disposable nappies, pays for it and goes towards the door.

'What a lovely baby!' Just in the doorway, an older woman is leaning over him, her mouth distorted into a kind of kiss. Her lipstick's bled into the surrounding skin. She bends over to tickle the baby under his chin. 'You're gorgeous, you are! Gorgeous! How old is he?' She straightens up and turns round. 'No, don't tell me. Let me guess. Fifteen weeks? Sixteen?'

'Eight days.'

'You're joking!' The woman laughs. 'Look at him! Come here, darling! Oh, I could eat you up!' She pushes her face at the baby and shakes her head rapidly from side to side, her nose almost close enough to touch his. 'Isn't your Mum silly? You're a real charmer, you are!'

'I had him eight days ago.'

'Well.' The woman looks at her with something like distrust. Or perhaps it's concern. 'I must say he's very big for eight days, love,' she says gently.

'I know.'

'And beautiful.'

'Yes.'

'Look...' She fumbles for something in her handbag. She finds it and snaps the gilt clasp shut – a small notebook. She scribbles something and tears out the page. 'There's nothing I don't know about babies. If you need to ask someone, that's where to find me. Solids, nappy-rash, teeth, you name it. I had six. All grown up now, and bigger than I am.' Her eyes stray to the plastic packet swinging from the handles of the buggy. She's reading the weights, doing her sums, still trying to work out what age the baby is. 'Fourteen weeks?' she says. She screws up her sun-ray mouth again.

Two days later he won't go in his crib without crying. Every time she tries to put him down he opens his mouth and starts to wail. He seems to be looking at her accusingly. And yet she's fed him. She lets him suck almost endlessly, until she can hardly stand up without feeling woozy. And in less than an hour she feeds him again.

And then she realises what the matter is. He's too big. He's growing out of the crib. When she puts him down on the mattress his head's squashed against the scratchy wicker surface, his feet flexed to make room, like someone lying in the bath. She picks him up and examines him. There's a red welt on his forehead, where he keeps looking up and straining and rubbing. And his feet have two angry-looking blisters. She puts the little basket crib away in the cupboard and gets out the full-size cot. She spends an hour fitting it together, cursing, not enough hands, the whole shaky structure leaning and threatening to fall sideways at any moment, wing-nuts spinning out from between her fingers and skidding across the floor.

When it's done she lowers the side and puts him in. It creaks under his weight. He looks up at her contentedly and then falls asleep. When he finally wakes and starts crying it's the middle of the night.

She leans over to lift him out. Anything to stop the screaming. But she can hardly manage it. He's a dead weight. She has to lift the sliding side of the cot right out and roll him towards her before she can get hold of him properly. And his clothes are gaping. The waist of his little velour trousers has worked its way down to his knees. And his top's pulled into such tight creases across his chest he can hardly breathe. She gets a pair of scissors and slits it from hem to neck.

*

A long metallic ringing cuts through her dreams. A fire-alarm – in her sleep she can already smell smoke, she's gathering her baby to her and running out into a street lit by jumping flames, waiting for the dark houses to crumble the moment she steps across the threshold. But it's only her doorbell. She sits up and pulls on a sweater. She goes to the door in her bare feet and opens it on its chain. She recognises the midwife, a thin section of face, collar, light mac, dark tights, shoe, visible in the gap. 'Just looking in on you, to make sure it's all going okay,' the mouth says.

She pulls her sweater down and moves away slightly, so the woman can't see she's in her pyjamas. 'We're fine,' she says.

'Really? No problems? That's wonderful!' In the crack the fabric of the mac moves slightly. 'Could I come in for a moment, do you think, just to have a little chat?'

'It's a bit of a mess.'

'Don't worry. I'm used to it. With a new baby, no one expects...'

Behind her he's beginning to wake up. She recognises the rhythmic creak and thump as he starts to pound with his legs against the bars. In a minute he'll open his mouth. She says, 'Hang on a moment...' She shuts the door on the woman and goes to his room. He's restless, waving his arms in a tangle of blanket, the cot a seething swell of flesh and pale blue wool. She slides the side down and kneels, her eyes on a level with his. She leans in and rests her head against his stomach and he seems to quiet, his arms no longer thrashing but almost still, his fingers opening and closing, discovering her face.

After a while the doorbell rings again. She feels her body tense. His seems to tense too under her. But she doesn't move. The bell goes again, a determined, protracted jangle. Then silence. After a few seconds she hears footsteps tapping away across the concrete, the lift shuddering down.

Now when she goes out she always goes alone. She leaves quickly, her head down, dodging between the kids in the entrance, not talking back. She half runs across the windswept grass to the little shopping arcade, grabs what she needs and hurries back. In the lift the words 'FAT PIG' are sprayed across the wall; the floors sink past in the crack between the steel doors.

But when she goes in he's still there, safe, not even crying, his wide eyes following the little clouds as they float across his window. When he catches sight of her he squeals and chortles and holds out his arms.

She's getting used to it, this whole strange business. She dresses him in her own clothes, uses towels for nappies. She's moved her own bed into his room for him, taken down the curtains to use as extra sheets. Every day she goes to the launderette, rushing back to feed him while the clothes are in the machine, kneeling on the floor beside him and leaning forward so he can take the nipple into his mouth. He's her baby. He's what she wanted. And he's perfect. When she bares his body little by little to wash him there isn't a single blemish anywhere. His skin's almost impossibly soft, the whites of his eyes so clear they're almost startling. She can bury her whole face in the shallow dip at the base of his plump neck. She inhales him slowly, as if she could just go to sleep, as if he'd never wake her again, fussing and flailing and crying to be fed.

In fact, these days he cries less. He lies looking at the sky outside, playing with his toes. And he makes sounds – long strings of nonsense syllables that go up the scale and down, like he's practising, waiting for the right person, the right moment, to deliver his first speech to an audience of strangers through the open door.

Then one night she's woken by a shriek. At first she can't tell whether it's from outside. There are people down there: a motorbike revs suddenly and roars away. There's a gasp of half-suppressed laughter – that must have been what woke her, kids outside under her window – or the noises she can hear coming from the baby's room.

Outside his door she listens till she hears the sound again. It's like someone trying to wake out of a bad dream. Something's bothering him. When she goes in, he's turning his head from side to side on the mattress, his arms and legs pumping. She sits on the floor at the head of his bed and tries to take him in her arms. He stops moving, attentive. And then she hears herself start to sing, shaky at first, almost under her breath – anything that comes into her head, everything she can remember, I'm a little teapot, incy wincy, abide with me. When he's finally asleep she covers him gently with the blanket. She kisses him on the forehead and tiptoes back to her own room.

Her own room is almost perfectly empty. No bed, no mattress, even. Only her sleeping-bag spread out across the floorboards, her dented pillow. She goes over to the uncurtained window and looks out. The kids have gone now. Just the odd small patch of oil glinting on the concrete, where their machines were standing. For once, the estate lights are out. There's only moonlight, making its sharp shadows, the colour all sucked out, and in the distance the line of dustbins just behind where the shops are, the quick streak and sudden eyes of a cat.

When she wakes the next morning, there's no sound. No crying. No strings of burbled vowels from her baby's room to her own. She goes out into the hall and stands for a moment with her hand on her baby's doorknob. She opens his door a crack.

And there he is, his eye open a few inches from hers, his cheek squashed into the sharp edge of the door, one arm up over his head, crumpled in the tiny space at the corner of the ceiling. He's having trouble breathing, the skin over his mouth already bluish. He's enormous. His face is five times the size of her own. He looks at her. He's wedged in so tightly there's nothing she can do.

She closes the door. In the hall she rummages for money, phone-numbers, a phone-card she's sure she put down somewhere. Then she pulls her coat on over her nightdress, pushes her bare feet into shoes and runs out on to the landing, stopping only a moment to lock the front door. She doesn't even wait for the lift to clank up from the ground to meet her. She half-falls down the stairs, her bare feet slipping inside the shoes so she almost trips, the graffiti a rainbow blur next to her face.

In the downstairs hallway, a couple of people are curled up in a corner, still sleeping under a grey blanket. Their dog gets up and walks towards her, quivering. Outside the sun shines straight in her eyes. She reaches the place in the middle of the grass where the two paths meet and cross in a square of chalked hopscotch. She steps over it and makes for the phone-box. Her teeth are chattering. Her jaw feels frozen, incapable of pronouncing even the simplest message. She pulls her coat round her and breaks into a run.

Acknowledgements

'Or' won a small prize in the 1998 Bridport competition under the title 'In Peace' and was published in the Bridport anthology of that year. 'Sharks' was first published in French as 'Voyage scolaire' in *Le Nord* magazine, July 1999. 'Roll Up for the Arabian Derby' appeared in the first edition of *Riptide* and 'Baby' in *Dream Catcher*.

I am very grateful for support from the Villa Mont-Noir Centre de Résidence pour Ecrivains Européens in North-East France, and particularly to the Virginia Center for Creative Arts where a number of these stories were written or revised.

I would also like to give very warm thanks to my first readers, Moniza Alvi, Mara Bergman, Bridget Collins, Caroline Price and Lynne Rees, and also to Philip Gross, Martin Scofield and Ali Smith for their valuable insights and encouragement. And thank you, Buddy, for the ventriloquist's dummy and the much-needed laughs.